# GIRL DIVIDED TWO

**SUZIE T. ROOS**

This book is a work of fiction. Names, characters, places, and incidents are the product of the author's imagination or are used fictiously. Any resemblance to actual events, locales, or persons, living or dead, is coincidental.

Girl Divided Two
Copyright © 2010, 2015 by Suzie T. Roos
ISBN No. 978-0-9962942-2-5

All rights reserved. No part of this book may be reproduced or transmitted in any form or by any means, electronic or mechanical, including photocopying, recording, or by any information storage and retrieval system, without permission in writing from the publisher.

Cover Photo Photographed and Backdrop Painting by Leroy Roper.

Model and Costuming by Tiffany Diamond

Art Direction by Suzie T. Roos

Cover Design and Interior format by
The Killion Group http://thekilliongroupinc.com

To my family: If it weren't for my husband, daughter and son, these books would not have come to life. Your love and support fuel what I write. We get to choose the path we take in life, and mine always had your names on it.

# ACKNOWLEDGEMENTS

Within six short months of my first release, *Girl Divided Two* is here, and it's all because of my awesome team.

Many thanks to my copy editor Amanda Sumner (Careful Copyediting), Marlo Berliner (Chimera Editing Services) for a great content edit, Dana Waganer for proofreading/editing, Lizzie Deal for proofreading, and Diana Drake for beta reading. Thank you all!

I couldn't have gotten *Girl Divided Two* over to my editorial team in time without my critique partners. Over a period of many weeks, they read through numerous chapters. Thank you Michelle Sharp, Linda Gilman & Claudia Shelton!

Thanks to Leroy Roper for the beautiful backdrop painting and the photography. And thanks to Tiffany Diamond for representing my heroine exactly the way I imagined her. This may be my favorite cover so far!!

Thanks to The Killion Group. I can't thank Kim Killion & Jennifer Jakes enough. You've helped me to establish my brand, get my books ready for their release, not to mention the many other tasks that go into getting a book published.

Last, but not least, thanks a million to my family . . . I love you three, G-V-J!

*Suzie T. Roos*

# CHAPTER 1

*Tatum*

I'd only ever wanted to be a "normal" teenager—what a joke. My life hadn't been normal in months. Of course, it would be hard to wish certain things hadn't happened, because after all I had the guy of my dreams.

Zacharia Nicola Bertano had asked me to be his girlfriend four weeks ago.

I could envision myself with him for the rest of my life. Of course, that meant I'd have to marry the Mob. Yup, the best guy any girl could wish for just so happened to be the grandson of an *ex*-Mob boss from Italy. For the moment, I was ignoring that minor hiccup.

Except that I owed Zach an answer to a larger question than whether I'd be his girlfriend—would I "speak for" him?

"Speak for"—that was committing to Zach without the ring on my finger, which wasn't a problem, but I'd have to commit to his family, too. A Mob family. This was not a decision to be made lightly. I was worried enough about that, but Zach also wanted me to meet his grandfather and his parents over the weekend.

I was having trouble picturing me, a girl who wore black combat boots with miniskirts and had the side of her head shaved, walking up to Mr. Ex-Mobster with my hand out. *Hello, Mr. Mobster Grandpa, I'm Tate* (it wouldn't be a good idea to tell him my last name) . . . *it's so nice to finally meet you.*

Who meets a mobster . . . *ever*? Zach said he'd been out of the business since they'd moved to St. Louis, but I'm no idiot—once you're in the Mob, you don't walk back out. I'd seen *The Godfather*—twice.

## Zach

Sometimes I hated being me, a Bertano. My family was a pain in the ass. We weren't a normal family. We were Mob . . . kind of. Gramps was an old-time Mob boss with one foot in the past and one in the here and now. It was his past that was causing me problems, because I was in love with Tatum Duncan. It only took me three years to become her boyfriend.

Tatum wasn't a girl you walked up to and started chatting with. But even before we'd ever really talked, I could see her strength and determination in those guarded eyes. Whether she knew it or not, she had qualities that would fit right in with my family.

In school, Tatum sat next to me at our lunch table. As usual, she and Andrea (Andi), who was dating my cousin Matt, were talking. Tatum was so beautiful. If only she'd realize how I would go to the ends of the earth for her. But to rush her into an answer would kill my chances. That's why she was clueless about the pressure my Gramps had been putting on me for the past month to get her to "speak for" me in return.

Gramps didn't accept the "just dating" commitment Tatum preferred. Gramps was old school—you commit, she commits, end of story. And it didn't matter if my father was Lead Man and my mother was Lead Woman. Here in the U.S., Gramps overrules everyone, even my Uncle Vito back in Italy. The only thing my parents could do for me was help stall. Tatum needed more time. Ironic, how similar Gramps and Tatum were.

Stubborn.

Pigheaded.

Determined.

When the bell rang and I walked Tatum to her fifth hour which was close to mine. Since her ex-boyfriend couldn't be trusted, I insisted on escorting her to every class.

I entered the boys' locker room and went straight to my usual locker of choice in the back corner. This part of the locker room was usually quiet by now with the previous class gone, but not today. Chatter coming from the row on the other side of the lockers and *his* fucking voice had me listening closer.

Kyle Wilson. Tatum's ex-boyfriend.

The jock who had dated her, cheated on her and raped her.

"That bitch walks around here with her nose up in the air with that fucking-lowlife-Italian's hands all over her. People only know Tatum because *I* dated her . . ."

No one else at Randall High boiled my blood the way he did. Hearing him call her a bitch had my hand clenching a fist. *Keep talking, Star Football Player . . . I'll show you what a lowlife Italian I can be.*

"She'll still get what she has coming to her," Kyle said.

I glanced around me; no one was on my side of the

lockers. I wanted to rush over there and snap Kyle's fucking neck. Because she was the one girl who wouldn't put out, she'd bruised his ego, and he couldn't take it.

The weight of my family's politics weighed on my chest. If Tatum only understood the protection she could get from this asshole if she'd speak for me.

"Kyle, shhh, keep your voice down. You know it echoes in here—"

That was his buddy, Aiden. Fine, I could take him too.

Aiden went on. "What do you mean, 'She'll still get what she has coming to her'? You honestly think we're stupid enough to fight the Bertanos again . . . over her? I have a football career to think about. If we get caught fighting, Coach will kick us off the team. You know his policy."

Damn it. Students filing in for the next class made it harder to make out what they were saying. I strained to hear every word.

"Idiot, there's other ways for her to get her due."

"What did Tatum ever do to you, Kyle? Besides, Bertano is with her every waking minute. He threatened to kill you the last time. I'm not sacrificing my football career for anyone, and neither should you," Aiden said.

The sound of a metal locker being caved inward momentarily silenced the locker room. "Big deal, he threatened me. He had to play the tough guy around his cousins. He doesn't scare me. Someway, somehow she'll get what's coming to her. And I won't need anyone's help," Kyle said. "Bertano can't be with her every waking—or sleeping—moment."

Without thinking, I slammed my fist into the locker, causing the row to vibrate as if they could go down like dominos. The prick was right about one thing. I couldn't be with her every minute, and that really pissed me off.

I threw my gym bag in a locker and stormed around the corner to face Kyle.

I stood there, crossing my arms over my chest. "Whatchya gonna do to Tatum, big bad Kyle?"

Aiden jumped and then took a step back, glancing around. Kyle didn't. He looked pissed that I'd caught him.

I kept my pleasure at startling them to myself. "Do you really think I, or anyone in my family, will let you within ten feet of her?"

Kyle flung his gym bag to the floor and got in my face. "Do you think you're going to stop me? I'm gonna do whatever I want. *You* don't scare me."

Aiden glanced around again. "Um . . . Kyle, let's go. I'm hungry." He placed his hand on Kyle's shoulder. "I said, let's go."

Kyle jerked his shoulder away from Aiden's hand. "I dare you to touch me again. This fool thinks he intimidates me." Kyle didn't take his eyes off of me, and his face was beet red. Just like Tatum always said, that was a sign Kyle had lost his shit.

A few spectators kept their distance.

I inched forward as far as I could go without touching Kyle and kept my voice down. "I'm going to tell you one time and one time only . . . you lay one of your tiny fingers on her, and I will fucking kill you." He had no clue who he was messing with, even if that was obviously a bluff. I jabbed my finger in his chest. "And so we understand each other . . . my family knows what you did."

Kyle's smug face contorted to panic. Yeah, that got

his attention.

"Hey, what's going on here?" Coach Henderson walked up. I respected the Tim Conway lookalike, but I wouldn't let him interfere.

Kyle backed up and snatched his bag from the floor. "Nothing. Aiden and I are going to lunch."

They walked off.

Aiden glanced back at me. Even though he mumbled, I could still hear him. "What is Bertano talking about, Kyle? His family knows what?"

Coach walked toward me. "Bertano? You okay?"

I could feel my chest heaving. "Sure, Coach. Just making sure Mr. Star Football Player knew what I was talking about."

Coach nodded. "Okay." He looked me up and down. "See you out on the floor in two."

No matter what I had to do, I'd be damned if I let that asshole touch Tatum again.

## CHAPTER 2

*Tatum*

"Mom, Zach's picking me up soon," I called from my bedroom.

Her footsteps pounded down the hall and she peeked her head through the doorway. "Be home on time, Tatum. Did you get all of your homework done?"

"Of course." I slid my arms in the jacket and adjusted my shoulders. "When am I ever late?" Her life's mission was to annoy me any chance she got. Any time I left the house, she felt the need to run through all of the house rules. As if I were some idiot who needed reminding every single frickin' day.

"Don't you think you guys are getting a little too close, too fast?"

Tact was my mother's middle name!

There's no way she would make me break up with him for "moving too fast." Nah. I spun around. Tossing my purse over my shoulder, I said, "No. Why? What's wrong with us?"

We hadn't done much. Just made out some, but of course she didn't know that.

She crossed her arms and leaned against the wall. "Oh, nothing. Nothing's wrong with you guys. Just that you spend every waking moment together." She glanced away and took in a breath. It was surprising to see her think before she opened her mouth. "Never mind. Be home after dinner. No going back to his house or anything like that."

Huh, she must not realize Zach enjoys St. Ferdinand Park—the local make-out point. Every teenager in the North County area goes there. And we spend every waking moment together because we love each other. "Got it. See ya later, Mom."

Saved by the rumble . . . I hustled out so Zach wouldn't have to deal with my mom too.

"That's probably him." I rushed past her. She followed me, closing my bedroom door behind her. Of course, a closed door never stopped her from snooping around.

My little sister, Toni, ran up to mom. "Mommy, Mommy, we have to walk Brittany home now," She pulled on mom's arm, clueless how she and her little friend from down the street saved me.

"All right. I'm coming, give me a minute," Mom said.

I hurried for the front door. "Bye, Dad."

Dad snorted, waking up from his recliner. "Oh, bye, Tate. Tell Zach to take care of my girl. Drive safe."

"Sure thing." I had to shut the door behind me fast so they wouldn't see me laughing. Zach would have loved hearing my father's request to take care of me.

The front door of Zach's '76 V8 four-speed Camaro opened, and I hopped inside. He greeted me with a warm kiss and dark sultry eyes. Done. I was cooked. Zach warmed me from head to toe. Damn . . . he was good.

Zach rested his elbow on the steering wheel, looking at me with that *GQ* face. "You ready to go eat, Tate?" But what his eyes were really asking was if we could make out instead.

Zach knew how to make me blush. I had to look away. This was one of many ways he flirted with me, but he could turn around and claim it was just a simple question. Nothing more.

"Yes!" I licked my lips and turned back to him. "You're bad, Zacharia, but you know I love it. Now drive, I'm hungry."

His signature Bertano smirk graced his face while he shifted in his seat. "Aye-aye, Captain. Thought we'd try this new Mexican restaurant down the street. You game?"

"Game if you are."

---

We were seated right away. Our waiter greeted us, then took our drink order and disappeared.

What was I in the mood for? Quesadillas? Or the usual tacos?

I could feel Zach's eyes on me, staring. I glanced up and met his gaze.

He had the darkest, sexiest eyes I'd ever seen. "So . . . since you don't work tomorrow night, I assume you're open to go with me? It's Friday night . . . I have to go to the Hill, Tate. Where my family meets for dinner."

Shit. That again.

Zach folded his hands on the table. His stare was obvious.

He was reading me, dang it. It wasn't a secret I'd

been avoiding this answer for days. Lately I'd been avoiding a lot of decisions that could lead into an even bigger decision. What if it was a trap? A trap to get me to "speak for" him?

*Look him in the eye and stop fidgeting.* "I am open. True. But I'm . . . to be honest . . . not sure—"

The waiter served our drinks and unloaded a basket of chips and salsa, then tucked the tray under his arm and asked if we were ready to order.

"Yes, we are. Tate?"

"I'll have the fish tacos. Thank you." I closed the menu and handed it over to the waiter.

"And I'll have the beef enchiladas."

A moment later, we were alone again.

"Tatum." Zach took my hands in his and placed them on the table. "Why don't you want to go? Be honest."

How could I tell Zach the truth without hurting his feelings? But he'd asked me point-blank.

He lowered his chin. Great. His patience was slipping. *I had to get out of this or my butt would be at the Mob restaurant tomorrow night.*

I took a deep breath. "Honestly . . . I'm a bit scared."

His mouth twisted in an unnatural way. Zach remained silent, clearly waiting for me to dig my hole deeper. He still held my hands, but didn't move.

"I mean . . . it's serious to meet anyone's family, Zach."

He rolled his tongue around on the inside of his mouth. Not amused. Not a good enough reason for him. Dang it. I rolled my head to get the kinks out of my neck. My hole was dug five feet—one more foot and that would be it for me.

"Okay. Fine. I'm scared of your grandpa." *Damn it.*

*That didn't come out right.*

He dropped my hands and sat back. "Why?"

I cocked my head to the side like a dog does. "What? You know why."

He leaned up against the table and glanced around us. "No. I don't. Tell me why, Tatum. And it wouldn't be wise to say the 'M' word." His face expressed that he wasn't playing around.

I too leaned against the table to better keep my voice down. "Because he controls everything in your family, so, right or wrong, I'm scared of him. Yes, because of the 'M' word, but too . . . because what if he's not impressed with me? All of your cousins know I was raped. So who else knows? It's embarrassing."

He took my hands. "Don't worry. That was not your fault. They would never hold anything like that against you. I promise."

"Good, but there's a lot of reasons he could disapprove of me. And the obvious . . . look at me, Zach." I leaned back and swished my hands down the front of me. "I know how I dress—"

He straightened his back. "What's wrong with how you dress? I love your eccentric look."

That made-to-order compliment comforted me. One of the many things I adored about him—he didn't give a damn what other people thought about us. I could have given in right then and there if he'd kept working that angle.

"Thanks. But we both know I'm not mainstream. I took a razor to the side of my head. Shaved the hair off—softer than a baby's butt. Sure, it's growing out, but still . . ."

Zach put his hand over that side of my head and gave the sweetest, softest smile. You could feel the warmth and love oozing from his hand. My breathing kicked up a notch.

He knew Kyle Wilson, the star football player at school, had raped me. And since Kyle loved my long hair, some of it had to go.

The truth was I trusted Zach with my life. He knew more about me than anyone else. I mean, he knew everything. So why would it be so scary for him to show me off? "So, you're saying you'd prance me in there on your arm? Announcing that I'm the one? No matter who I am or what has happened to me, I'm the one? That puts a lot of pressure on me."

He rubbed the side of my head and then let go. "The beauty of my family is that they're to respect my decision no matter who I decide is *the one*, as you call it. You know how much I love you. I'd give my life for you without blinking. You don't have to feel that way for me, not yet—"

"Hold up . . . don't you think the feeling is mutual?"

"If it is, Tate, then why can't you say those words? I. Love. You."

"I can." I had to look away. Why couldn't I say those words to him, when the thought of him or the mention of his name sent my heart into a fifty-meter dash? But then what was the next step? We'd both tell each other the extent of our feelings? We'd kiss. We'd cuddle . . . then what? Zach was so intense. Things would escalate.

The server arrived with our dinner plates and placed our meals in front of us. The aroma of cilantro, tomatoes and corn tortillas flooded my senses.

I looked up at our waiter. "Looks perfect. Thanks!"

He bowed and walked off.

I took my first bite of fish tacos when I glimpsed at

Zach's posture—tense and taut.

"Don't think this is over. We'll talk about it after you eat. And about the fact that you won't meet my family."

"Fine," I said, giving him my best pouty face.

My hesitation to say *I love you* could be hurting his feelings too. I loved him more than anything. Zach had made it clear that whether I said I loved him or not, he'd die for me. Why was this so complicated? "Can I ask you something?"

He took a bite of his meal, but paid attention.

"Actually, there's a lot I'd like to ask."

He grinned. "Go ahead, but I know where this is going."

That man was so confident. "Okay, smarty pants, then get ready to answer this. What will happen if I go down there with you tomorrow?"

He finished chewing and sat up. "We'll eat. Then after dinner, Gramps will speak to everyone. When he's finished talking, you'll introduce yourself. They usually socialize after dinner for a while, then we go home. It's just dinner."

That didn't sound so bad.

Zach put his fork down. "Look, Gramps stays in his office most of the time. You seriously would just have to say hi at the table. Otherwise, it's low-key."

It's his grandpa. How would I feel if he were afraid to meet my grandma if she were alive? I'd be crushed. Of course, she wasn't in the Mob. All the same, she's my blood. And I'd want to show Zach off to her and the rest of my family. I honestly believe she would have liked my boyfriend. *Damn . . . I'm pretty lucky. Just look at him . . . he has everything going for him. What could be the worst thing to happen tomorrow?*

Why risk hurting his feelings?

"Zach, I've been think—"

His mobile rang. Zach was the only one I knew who had the new MicroTAC Motorola flip phone. He reached for his jacket, grabbed his mobile and extended the tiny antenna

He never got mobile calls when we were out.

"Yeah." His eyes met mine for a split second before looking away again. "Are you serious?" He took a few deep breaths.

He covered his mouth with his other hand, buffering his speech. "Yes. I understand. I'll need a few extra minutes . . . Tate's with me. I know." His face was red. "I said, I understand." Then he snapped the phone shut and wouldn't look at me.

"Is everything okay?"

He wiped his mouth with the napkin and dropped it onto his plate. "We gotta go."

"Right now?"

"I'm sorry, but we need to leave."

"Uh . . . are you serious?"

"Yes. Now." He scooted out of the booth.

"We just got our food—"

He jerked toward me and went to smack his hand on the table, but stopped. He bit his lip and took a deep breath. "Tate, I need to leave right this minute. And you're not being left behind. So we're both leaving. Now."

The waiter showed up. "Sir, is there something wrong?"

"No. But will you box her food? We need to leave right away."

He nodded and rushed off.

Zach yanked his jacket from the booth's bench and

tossed it on, removing his wallet. His eyes changed. They were serious. Like they were the night I told him what Kyle had done to me.

"Is someone hurt? Is your mom and dad okay?" I asked, hurriedly collecting the food I wanted to take home, realizing Zach was leaving. He meant it.

He took a fifty-dollar bill out of his wallet. "Yes, they're fine. Don't worry."

The waiter came running back and immediately boxed my food. Zach gave him the fifty. "Muchas gracias. Keep the change."

The waiter's eyes widened at the fifty dollar bill. "Thanks."

Zach put his hand out for me. "Tate. Now."

I took his hand, but not without a scowl. "I'd like to know—"

"Wait till we get in the car."

Zach was speed-walking across the parking lot. Everything was happening so fast. A million things were going through my head, all in slow-motion. *We're dropping everything for what? I'd like to know. This has to be serious.* Zach unlocked my door and flung it open. By the time I'd wedged my leftover dinner between my feet and secured my seat belt, his keys were shoved in the ignition. He floored the gas and peeled out of the parking lot.

"Okay, can you tell me what's going on now? You're scaring me."

Zach stayed focused on driving. "I'm being summoned by my family."

"Summoned? What the hell? We were having—"

"One of my uncles might be in trouble. Try to understand. Please, Tate."

He still didn't look at me. I could see his jaw

clenched from where I sat.

"Sorry. Is he hurt?"

"No. Look . . . I'm not sure what's going on myself." Zach patted the inside of my leg—a small token of affection to let me know he wasn't mad at me. But that did not make this okay. He was clearly stressed, breathing fast, and not looking at me. For the first time in our relationship, my boyfriend was in a hurry to get me home.

Whatever was happening to his family was not good. Zach had never been curt with me. My stomach was knotting so badly it felt as if someone were in there making dough. I was scared.

Maybe we could drive away, skip town for a day or two. I didn't want to lose him. *Maybe I'm overreacting again. Whatever it is wouldn't go that far. Right? I think so, but his actions are scaring the shit out of me.*

Moments later, we were hauling ass down my street. "Zach, could you please slow down just a bit? If my parents hear you coming—"

"Of course. Sorry."

The problem with a big V8 engine was that you could hear us coming a mile away.

Zach slowed to a stop in front of my house and shifted into neutral.

Reaching for my to-go bag, he said, "Here, hon. I'll call ya later if I can."

*That's it? Dismissed from our date like that? This sucks.* He leaned over and kissed me on the lips.

Pressing past me, Zach flipped open my door.

That made it loud and clear—get out. *Could this be a sign? Am I losing him?*

I looked him straight in the eye, trying not to cry. His handsome face distracted me, but there was no denying he was miles away. Selfish, but I had to have him there with me for a second, for this moment. "I. Love. You. Zacharia."

His eyes expanded and his mouth dropped open.

He heard me.

"I love you more than anything. Please be safe." Then I pulled his head toward mine and gave the guy I loved one heck of a kiss.

Zach leaned back and bit his lip. He took a breath and grinned. "Now you tell me—" He cupped the side of my face. "I have to go. God knows I wish I didn't, but I do."

I didn't waste another second getting out. With a bag of fish tacos in my hands, I waved goodbye to the guy I loved with all my heart.

## CHAPTER 3

*Tatum*

My mother thought she was seeing things, doing a double take when I walked in the front door forty five minutes after I left.

Dad spun around in his recliner. "Hey, didn't you just leave?"

Mom's attention went straight to the doggie bag. Then her glare met mine. She suspected we'd had a fight.

At least if we'd had a fight I would have known why my butt was back home.

I walked past them, heading to my bedroom. "I did. Zach got called away. Something came up."

With a slight kick of my foot, I closed the bedroom door behind me. Privacy was hard to come by ever since my mother had made me move my bedroom upstairs. All to better watch over me and my boyfriend. I flipped on the TV and dropped my jacket and purse on the corner chair. Having dinner in bed alone was not my idea of a great night out with Zach.

With a bloated belly from a great Mexican dish, I realized my evening sucked. An hour and a half had passed since Zach had dropped me off. Why would he get called away to help one of his uncles? How could Zach help him? What kind of help did he need?

"Tatum? Tate, come here. Quick," Mother yelled from the living room.

My head whipped in the direction of her panicked voice. I flung the blankets off and damn near tripped, grabbing the door and flinging it open. Even with noodle legs, I ran in. "What?"

Mom pointed to the TV, her eyes as big as jawbreakers and her mouth hanging open.

A newscaster's voice buzzed, ". . . while moments ago, Sergio Bertano was taken in for questioning about an international money-laundering case. Police have a warrant for his computer and any files in his home."

There, walking up the courthouse steps, was a very tall, strong-looking Italian man wearing all black. He didn't seem to have a care in the world. Three men walked behind him wearing lawyer-type suits and carrying briefcases. This Sergio looked confident, whereas the suits looked pissed off.

A cinder block landed on my chest, causing erratic breathing. *Do not tell me this is the uncle. Please.* Zach had said something happened to one of his uncles. This could be why he'd been "summoned" and had to drop everything, including me. This had to be why he got "summoned."

I carefully scanned the crowd for familiar faces, like Zach's. No one looked familiar, but I recognized Sergio's smug smirk. It was the spitting image of Zach's. I didn't want to believe that he was family, but looking at the man, I couldn't deny the resemblance.

Dad shifted in his recliner. "Tate, they said Sergio Bertano . . . of Bertano's Restaurant and Catering on the Hill. Is this one of Zach's uncles? What's his father's name?" Dad asked.

*Shit. Bertano's Restaurant? This can't be happening.*

My tongue was tied and I couldn't move, not even my head. The resemblance . . . not just to Zach . . . but to his cousin. "I don't know if that's his uncle. But his father's name is Nicola." My words came out hushed.

"Oh my Lord . . . look at the lawyers, Ken. This is serious. Tatum, have you heard from Zach since he dropped you off?"

"No." I couldn't take my eyes off the TV.

One of the attorneys turned around and stopped the media from following further. The reporter shoved a microphone in his face.

"Does Mr. Bertano have connections to Switzerland?" one newswoman asked.

"What evidence do they have against your client?" another reporter shouted out.

That got the lawyer's attention. "None. They have no evidence against my client. He has not been arrested, nor has he been charged. Now . . . if you would give Mr. Bertano the courtesy of not being treated like a criminal, we'd appreciate it. Thank you." He walked off, even more pissed.

The camera cut back to the first reporter. "Reporting live from the federal courts downtown, I'm Laurie Summers. John, Spencer . . . back to you in the newsroom."

"Thanks, Laurie." The camera focused on one guy behind the desk. "We'll keep you posted on any development in that story."

They moved on to the weather.

What a relief Zach wasn't there. Or if he had been, I

hadn't seen him in the dark.

"Tatum, we should talk," my dad said.

"About what?" I replied, still not taking my eyes off the TV. For some reason, my imagination was scanning all of Sergio's features.

Mother let out an obnoxious huff. "About your boyfriend. Now, he wasn't on TV, but that appeared to be his family. Tatum, we do not need to get wrapped—"

"We don't know who that was." I jerked my head toward her. I felt my nostrils flaring as I continued to yell, "Bottom line. Did you see Zach? No."

"Tate, calm down. What your mother is trying to say—"

"I heard what she said." I practically snapped my neck whipping my head around so fast. "She's going to make me break up with him because that may—or may not—have been his uncle. So what if it was? What if he never talks to him? You and Mom both have family you don't talk to. So don't—"

"Tatum. Calm down. And stop yelling at us." My dad took a deep breath and relaxed his shoulders. "Look . . . find out what's going on. I'm pretty sure that's an uncle of Zach's. What they're taking him in for is very serious, Tate. Very serious. But you know that."

"I know." Another hushed response.

"Have you even considered how this affects you?"

"Me? No. What do you mean?" I wasn't sure what Dad was getting at, but by his heavy breathing and sighing, his patience was wavering.

"Since you're dating one of them, the police could pull you in for questioning. That's how they work. They question everyone in the suspect's circle."

"I don't know anything. I've never even met his

family." My heart pounded so fast it hurt my chest. The police? Questioning? My thoughts went straight to a small, dreary-looking room with a one-way mirror. I couldn't even say what his family looked like, except his cousins.

"Talk to him. But remember, Tate, you're young and have a lot of options in your life. If that is Zach's family, and I'm betting my salary it is, he may not have as many options. Trust me, I like the guy. So does your mother. But in the end, we only have your best interest at heart." Dad inclined his head. "Try to get some sleep."

I flopped down on my bed and stared up at the ceiling, tears only a short distance away. My Jack Russell terrier, Gizmo, jumped up next to me.

*Poor Zach. Where could he be?* The urge to call his mobile was crippling. I didn't trust myself, so lying there and not moving seemed like the smartest thing to do. Who wants to come off as the overprotective girlfriend?

Gizmo nudged his wet nose against my arm. Amazing how dogs can read your emotions. "Don't worry, buddy. I'll be fine . . . just worried about Zachy." Zachy—I thought that was a cute pet name for my boyfriend. Zach didn't seem as convinced when he heard it.

Gizmo whimpered and put his head down on my stomach. We were both worried.

How did my life go to shit with one phone call? I wasn't ready to meet his family, but was this necessary?

If only I could hear his voice telling me everything was okay. I couldn't take not hearing from him.

*Just go to sleep. Stop thinking about it. You'll get to see him in the morning.*

I was almost asleep when the phone on my nightstand rang. Without thinking, I jerked the phone off the receiver. "Hello?"

Before the person could answer, my mother picked up. "Hello?"

"Um, hi, Tate. It's Di."

The relief washed over me. It wasn't the cops. I could breathe again. There were only a couple of people I could trust with such subject matter, and Diane was one of them. We'd met in seventh grade and had become best friends that first day of school. Like Zach, she was Italian.

"Don't be on long, Tate." Mother hung up.

"Oh my God, Tate. Did you see the news?" Diane sounded out of breath. That made two of us.

"Unfortunately. I take it you did too?"

"Unfortunately, I think most people did. Have you talked to him yet?"

"No. And now my mom and dad are telling me about how I have options in life."

"Are they going to make you break up with him?"

"Who knows? All I know is a big fat nothing."

She was quiet for a moment.

"Take it from me, Tate . . . keep it that way."

---

Lucky for me, my neighbor friend, Christy—a tall brunette with nicer hair than a Dallas Cowboys cheerleader—didn't mention the news broadcast on the bus. Starting a day with her giving me twenty questions was never fun. And she wouldn't think twice about drilling me until my ears bled.

The moment our bus came to a stop in front of the

brick box they called Randall High School, I hightailed up the front steps. My skills at dodgeball paid off as my short legs zigzagged through the crowd of socializing students. I had to get to our locker. Zach should be there. If only I could see over the heads to make this search faster.

It sucked being short.

Someone brushed my shoulder.

"Stop," Di whispered. She grabbed my arm and jerked me back to her.

My arm was still attached . . . "What the hell, Di? I'm sorry, but I haven't seen Zach yet. I have to go." My breathing was heavy, panting, as if I were a winning greyhound.

She didn't let go of my arm. "Yeah, I know. But you won't find him at your locker. He's with his cousins."

"What?" He was never at his cousins' locker.

"Follow me." She pulled my arm in the opposite direction.

"If you know anything, just spill it, Di. I'm sick of being the last one to get the news."

I didn't know if I should hold my head high or duck down like Zach does with everyone in the hall watching us and whispering to each other. It was clear from all of the gawking students that we weren't the only ones who watched the news.

"Simple. I ran into your boyfriend after he arrived this morning. He got sidetracked, and now his cousins are with him." She looked back at me with raised eyebrows.

Great. The look that says, *something else happened.*

Diane glanced around and huffed. "Ignore these assholes. And I'd get used to people goggling at you like you're a cyclops till this whole thing blows over."

Let them gawk, I thought. How people saw me at school was the least of my worries. I held my head high and let Diane escort me to Zach. We turned into the hall that encircled the cafeteria. Nothing but lockers lined the dark brick walls.

One thing immediately caught my attention: Matt—Zach's enormous cousin and Andi's boyfriend, who stood well over six feet three inches tall.

Diane turned back to me. The retro black frames she'd taken from her father caught my attention. Easy to see the pity in her eyes with the Coke-bottle lenses removed. "He's over there." She dropped my hand and pointed to where Matt stood. "And don't worry about his hand. I'm sure Catalina will take care of it tonight."

*What? Is Zach hurt?* I ran toward Zach before saying thanks to Di.

Making it around the crowd, I finally spotted him. His tall, lean body rested casually against the lockers. My heart stopped, as did my breathing. The only part of my body that was working was my chest—or at least, that was the only thing I felt.

All of his Bertano cousins were there. Tyler and Matt backed up, letting me reach my boyfriend.

Zach looked up at me, and you could see the heartbreak written all over his face. I scanned his body. He was in one piece except for his left hand, which he held. He tucked the puffy hand up against his torso, protecting it.

Fine, just his hand, we could deal with that. Relief helped ease the ache in my chest from not knowing if he was okay or not. And thankfully he was. I flung myself forward and collided with him. Zach wrapped his arms around my body, squeezing me into him.

"Oh Zach, what happened? Are you okay?" I backed

up and examined his face. Tired, droopy eyes exposed his fatigue.

His good hand lifted my chin. Those perfect, warm lips came toward mine. Immediately, sparks ran along our lips.

"Hon, I'm fine. Ignore my hand."

"What happened to it?" I pulled away to stop pushing him into the lockers. That's when I noticed his cousins were circling us, giving us privacy from the gawkers.

I stepped in, whispering, "We need to talk."

"Sorry. Not here. Too many ears. I'll come to your house after school."

"Just answer this . . . was that your Uncle on TV last night? Serg—"

"Yes. Shhhh." Zach put his index finger over my lips.

Bobby had walked up next to me. Our shoulders touched, but he wouldn't look at me. "Tate, it would be best to talk about my dad later." He looked me straight in the eyes. "Things are complicated in the family at the moment."

I knew it. Sergio was Bobby's dad. But the satisfaction of knowing I'd called the connection was short-lived. Even with Bobby's attempt at a grin, heartbreak was in his sorrowed eyes. I lightly touched his shoulder. What an awful feeling for someone to see their father called in for questioning by the police. "Of course. I'm sorry."

Zach grasped my hand and stepped away from the lockers. "Let's go get what you need for class. We'll walk and talk."

But we weren't alone. Matt followed closely behind us. I turned around and he gave me a silent nod with a stony expression, then began watching the halls.

Zach draped his arm around my shoulder, pulling me close. "Sorry. Tyler doesn't want me alone right now."

"Why? Because of your uncle?"

He glimpsed down at me. "Don't assume this is all about him. When I got here this morning, some asshole popped off." Zach shrugged. "We might be family, but my cousins don't have a temper like I do."

I couldn't believe my ears. Did he honestly attack someone? At school?

"No one talks about my family, Tate, and gets away with it."

"I get it, but are you telling me you socked someone because they—"

"I said, no one." His eyes pierced mine, then he took a breath and glanced around. "Just ignore everyone staring. God only knows how many saw the news last night."

Walking with the Bertanos drew more attention than walking with Diane had. The three of us were watched as if we were painted green and wearing rubber scuba suits.

I squeezed Zach's hand. We were in this together. Not sure what we were in, but Zach was technically fine. He was comfortably back in my arms.

The only thing I could ask for was the comfort his touch provided. I placed my head on his shoulder, needing his touch, a perfect touch.

"I love you, Zach."

"Hon, if only you knew how much I love you." He gave a sincere squeeze.

We looked at each other and his eyes gave me security—something Zach had always made me feel. Not sure how, but everything would be okay between us. It just had to be.

## CHAPTER 4

### Zach

I pulled behind my mother's car in the back of Bertano's on the Hill after school. Gramps insisted we park in back during business hours. Security cameras covered each corner of the brick building, along with motion sensors. Every second of the day, he had his eyes on all sides of the restaurant, always watching what was going on around him. Paranoid old man.

Showtime. Walking into the family's private entrance, I took a deep breath and stood tall.

"Oh, Zacharia." My mother came running over to me.

"Hey, Mom."

She pulled me in for a quick hug before backing away.

Mom whispered, "Gramps is waiting for us. You know what to do. I'm feeling good about this."

It was no secret in my family that my mother, Catalina—Cat for short—had strong intuition. Like Tatum.

Our family used a private wing of the restaurant that

led to Gramps's office. The hall displayed Gramps's love for dark wood and intricate carpentry. This was his second home.

Mother gave the solid mahogany door three knocks. This was a specific signal to announce the family.

"Come in," Gramps called out.

We walked into his office, a den he'd spent a lot of money to soundproof, making the space picture-perfect enough for *Architectural Digest*. The room was complete with built-in shelves, a wet bar, and a cozy sitting room for Grandma Cecilia. Gramps looked comfortable wearing his standard three-piece pinstriped suit, his black hair with minimal gray combed straight back, sipping a dark cocktail behind his enormous desk. An enormous desk for an enormous guy—he may have been an old man, but Gramps was a solid six feet four.

"*Ciao*, Zacharia . . . *sedersi*." He motioned to the two chairs in front of him.

Mother took the second chair.

Gramps put his drink down, folded his sleeves up, and then placed his forearms on his desk, leaning forward. He was ready to do business. "First, thank you for helping Sergio and Baldassario wipe their computer. Nicola should be returning with Sergio any moment. *Grazie*."

Hearing Gramps thank me for what I did put an annoying prick in the back of my throat. Thank god Tatum didn't know anything about that because if she did, I could kiss the possibility of her speaking for me goodbye.

Gramps continued. "So, now . . . you here to talk about this girl you spoke for . . . Tatum? What can I do?"

With his thick accent, he couldn't pronounce

"Tatum" like Americans do. It came out like "Tahtoom." I'm not sure Tatum would recognize her own name coming from a true Italian tongue. "You're welcome. And yes, sir. It's about Tatum."

Gramps wasn't an easy man to approach, let alone persuade to do something to help another. One foot in front of the other . . . "Sir, I ask that certain precautions be put in place to protect my spoken for right now." I leaned back, hands cupping the chair arms, calming my breathing.

One of his dark eyebrows shot upward. "What kind of protection do you ask? You've already committed yourself to her, what else?"

Mother glanced over at me. I imagined her saying, "Just say it, Zacharia. Ask him."

"Honestly?"

Gramps nodded.

"There's a guy who won't leave her alone . . . he's bound to hurt her. I overheard him telling friends I couldn't be with her every waking or sleeping moment. I just have a feeling he'll try getting to her from her bedroom window while she sleeps. It's in the front corner of her house."

"Who is this boy?"

Damn it. I didn't want to tell him about Kyle. But he would never help if he didn't know. "Her ex-boyfriend."

Gramps sat back. "Zacharia, I have no time for jealous ex-boyfriends. You know what this family is going through right now."

Exactly the reaction I'd known I'd get. "I understand, but could we put a camera on Tate's bedroom windows? Something? I'm not asking for much." Sounding desperate would not be productive with Gramps. Gramps was a caring man, but he had always expressed how he did not want to see his family show any weakness, of any kind.

He laughed so loudly it startled me. "Not much? You know Sergio can't touch our security right now. And I'm not letting Baldassario stick his neck out either. Has this girl even said she'll speak for you?"

"No. Not yet." God knows I was trying, though.

My mother adjusted herself in the chair. "Gramps, I know it sounds silly to you, but this girl does love Zach. It wouldn't be much for us to keep an eye on her."

"No." Gramps pulled a cigar out of his humidor and cut the tip off before lighting up.

"Sir?" I could feel the sweat beads form on my forehead. "I can do it myself. I'll put the cameras in place. Anything to protect her."

"Why are you so scared of this boy, Zacharia?"

"I'm not." *Great, is that what he thinks? Me afraid of Kyle? That's a joke. I could have killed him if I wanted instead of dislocating his shoulder the last time, I just held back.*

Gramps appeared to have not one iota of stress or concern. If only I felt the way he looked.

"I say no. I don't understand what it is with you and this Tatum."

"I love her."

"Why, give me one damn good reason she needs help. The Bertano family is top priority. Not some German teenager that'll move on to the next boyfriend in a few months. Does she even know who we are? Have you been honest with her? I'm not—"

"She was raped," I shouted. Tatum didn't know I exposed her secret, so why did I feel like I'd betrayed her? I had to tell him, though. Hearing anyone talk about her as if she were some tramp pissed me off.

Gramps melted back into his chair, not saying a word. Silencing him was a first.

"By who, Zach? That ex of hers?" Mother asked.

"Yeah. That fuck-head. And if that weren't enough, he's threatening to do more. He hates that Tatum is with me. I feel like she's just a sitting duck."

Mother stared into her lap and patted my shoulder.

"I'm sorry to hear that," Gramps said.

"Then help me, help her. I spoke for her. We should be protecting everyone who is spoken for in the family. I thought that was the rule?"

"I'm sorry this Tatum has suffered. But do not question my authority."

Mother moved her hand down to my arm. "No, Pops, he wouldn't do such a thing. But we know young love. Like I've said, I've seen this girl in our future. Give her time to speak for my son in return. Especially if she's been through that. Meanwhile, let Zach protect her the best way he sees fit."

Damn . . . Mom really stuck her neck out for me. I placed my hand over hers. She grinned, but kept her eyes on Gramps.

Gramps looked at her as if he were deciding how to dismantle a shelf. "I'll be damned if we risk ourselves for anybody outside the family right now. Bottom line. She hasn't, and won't speak for you. There's other fish in the sea. Lots of choices." When Gramps was sincere about something, he bopped his hand up and down. "Like good Italian girls that understand how families work."

Mom crossed her legs. "I told you before, Gramps, that won't work."

I looked at them, they both wore death glares. "You

said what won't work, Mom?"

She released my arm and shot her hand up, silencing me.

Gramps leaned forward, taking a quick puff. "Davide and I have talked. He's older than I and quickly tiring. He wants to be reassured his empire will be in good hands. We've talked about you and your ability to lead, Zacharia. I see the potential you have. With my help, you can take his empire over if you marry Mariacella. She's grown and ready to speak for—"

"Mariacella? I thought we were trying to cut ties to families like that?" I asked.

Mother looked at me. "You remember playing with her as a child? She's grown now, and Gramps was cutting ties, until Davide reached out to him." Mother turned to Gramps. "I was also under the impression we had to keep a low profile."

"Nah." This was absurd. "Princess?" I had to stop myself from laughing at the most ridiculous idea ever. "Sorry, Gramps, but I could never be with a girl like that, I'd rather—"

"You're wrong, my grandson. That's exactly the kind of girl you need in this family. A strong Italian woman. Now, you may think you're in love with this German, but once you're in good company with an Italian woman, you'll see this is all—"

He was serious. "No. Not her." I panicked. "Mom?"

Mariacella was known by many families to be a terrible princess. She'd grown up, all right. She was demanding, selfish, irrational—all traits Gramps was aware of but ignored. Davide would do anything for his daughter, and she knew it. Gramps wouldn't push me into any kind of relationship with Princess just because he wanted Davide's empire too. *Would he? He'd go that far?*

Mother sat perfectly straight with her legs crossed, and the top leg bounced up and down. "Zach's Tatum is stronger. Mariacella doesn't compare to *his German*. I've told you over and over, I have seen Tatum in our future. And for the last time, *it won't work*." She looked at me. "Zach, I'm sorry. But Tate can't get the extra protection right now. You'll have to figure something else out. Let's go."

She stood up and stepped around the chair. I followed my mother's lead—exactly what we were to do in this family. My mother was the Lead Woman in the U.S. She had more power and say than any other woman in the entire family.

## CHAPTER 5

*Tatum*

After spending all day with Zach, you would think I'd know more than I had when I'd gotten out of bed. Nope. I knew he was under a lot of stress, but I'd never seen him with such little patience and such an unpredictable temper.

As if my stomach wasn't flipping around like a dolphin already, the idea of meeting the whole Bertano clan tonight made my stomach feel even sicker. Thus the reason I ate my mom's entire bottle of Rolaids.

Zach already had bigger issues to deal with. Like his uncle. The uncle who could cause everyone to be taken into the police station for questioning. Or at least that's what my dad had feared would happen to me.

The fact was, half of the day was gone and I still knew nothing.

Time to put my big-girl pants on and at least meet his parents or whoever would be there.

I glanced at the clock—five thirty. Zach had said he would be by after my family left for dinner. They'd left half an hour ago.

This couldn't be over soon enough. All I hoped for

was that Zach and I could be together and move on.

The low rumble of a V8 engine came from outside.

I greeted him at the door. "Hey, Zachy."

"Must you call me that?"

Zach looked so handsome walking up my driveway, wearing all black, his hair a wind-blown mess. "Yes, I must."

He rolled his eyes, and that's when something along the front of my house caught his attention. Zach's gaze narrowed, toward my bedroom window.

"What?" I followed his glare. What could be so interesting about my mom's dead flower bed?

"Nothing. It's nothing." He stepped up on the threshold and gave my cheek a soft kiss for an entry fee. The best way to greet me.

In my bedroom, Zach sat on the side rail of my queen-size waterbed. He quickly lost his balance, and the sloshing sent him flat on his back with a loud smack against the rubber mattress. I couldn't help but laugh at him. He looked as if he'd just flipped off a skateboard. And all my boyfriend did was sigh, staring up at the ceiling.

Poor Zach was defeated by a waterbed.

"You'll get used to it." I chuckled.

Zach whipped his head at me with a *where-am-I* look.

"The waterbed." I nudged my head. "It becomes quite relaxing, once you get used to it." *Shit . . . no wonder he gave me that look. Did I just invite him into my bed?*

The Bertano signature smirk smoothly graced his face—a little too smoothly.

Getting back to what I was doing before he arrived, I picked up the clear packing tape from my dresser and pulled the window curtain back.

"I look forward to getting used to it, Tatum. But not today." He rolled out of bed and walked toward me with a sparkle in his eyes.

I agreed. Now was not the time to think about making out with him. The screen had to be fixed before my parents noticed. This wasn't a one-person job, though. "Zach, could you hold this screen together while I tape it?"

He stepped up to the window and looked down, directly into the garden. He looked at me. "What happened? Did you rip this?"

Tension was rolling off of him in waves. I leaned back. "No, why would I do that? I was watching out for you just now, and that's when I noticed it. Why are you acting mad at me?"

His shoulders dropped and his eyebrows relaxed as he slightly shook his head. "I'm sorry. I'm not mad at you. Here—" Zach reached for the tape. "You hold it and I'll tape."

I lined up the screen the best I could. He ripped off a piece of tape and sealed the rip back together.

To the naked eye, it was unnoticeable. Now my parents wouldn't accuse Zach of trying to sneak in, which was exactly what it looked like had happened.

Zach put the tape on my dresser and turned back to me. "I want these windows kept locked."

"What? Why?" I would swear someone had invaded my boyfriend's body, because this was not *my* Zach.

"Tatum, I don't ask much from you—"

The hell he didn't, speaking for him wasn't much? "Okay. What is going on? This isn't like you."

He took a deep breath and stepped up to the window, made sure it was shut all the way, and then locked it.

"Nothing's going on."

I tugged on his arm, pulling him away from the window. "Stop. Are you upset because of my screen?"

"Yes."

"Why? Gizmo probably did it. He hops in my bed and stands at the window, barking out. Don't worry, I'll make sure my parents won't think you did it. I'm more worried about mosquitos getting in."

Zach held my shoulders. "Keep Gizzie in bed with you at night."

We had bigger problems to worry about than a stupid ripped screen. Zach still owed me answers. Like what was happening with his Uncle Sergio. *Maybe if I changed topics things would calm down between us.*

"Your hand looks better than it did this morning." It did. The swelling was gone and it wasn't tomato red.

Zach examined the morning's injury, stretching his fingers out and in. "Yeah. It's fine."

"No one's here. Why don't you tell me why you got summoned last night?"

He leaned his backside against my dresser and crossed his arms over his chest. "First, my Uncle Sergio is not being charged. But as you saw, he was taken in for questioning. That's why I got summoned."

"Not sure I follow. Do you know if he's staying out of jail? The attorney made it clear last night there weren't any charges yet."

"He's not being charged because they don't have any evidence, so he should stay out of jail. The computer was cleaned."

*The computer was cleaned. Why?* "Tell me he's not guilty."

Wearing the same confident smirk as his Uncle Sergio had on the news, Zach said, "No, he's not guilty."

He blinked, fast. His lips tightened and he stared right through me.

Not the reaction I expected. Typically, when someone looks you in the eyes, especially one who claims to love you, they don't lie. But I'd bet money Zach did.

Neither one of us said a word for what felt like an hour until he ran his hand through his hair and began pacing. "Tonight's off—"

"Off . . . why?" Not that I minded.

Zach huffed, "Because of the situation. Why can't you just accept that I have a family?" He stared at me, emotionless. Hands on his hips.

I stood up, even though he appeared unapproachable. "Zach, I do. I'm not sure where this is coming from."

"It comes from you not understanding I have certain responsibilities in my family."

"I completely understand about commitments to your family. None of this tells me why *you* had to be there. And where's 'there'?"

"The Hill. And if you must know, my father wanted me with my mother while he and Piero took a trip."

I stepped closer to him. "Sorry. I don't know who Piero is?"

"Another uncle. He's Matt's dad. He's actually the baby in my father's generation."

"How many uncles do you have?"

"I have three uncles. Vito is the oldest son. He lives in Italy and is a Lead there. His job is to keep Gramps's enterprise alive in Italy. Then Sergio is the second-oldest son. But he's not a Lead, my dad is. My dad is the third son. Then Piero is the baby."

Gramps had four sons? That sounded like a lot of

testosterone in one family. I was getting somewhere, but my gut, or his facial expression, told me not to press my luck. Move on. "Okay, so who's Catalina?"

He hadn't looked at me much, but that got his attention. "How did you hear that name?"

"Today, when Di took me to your cousins' lockers. She said not to worry about your hand because Catalina would look at it."

Zach's face formed into a gentle grin. "Catalina is my mother. The family calls her 'Cat'. Like, as in a leopard. She's discreet and lethal at the same time."

"That's a beautiful name." I glanced up at him. He spoke so softly about his mother.

Zach relaxed his backside up against the dresser again. I didn't feel as much tension between us. His temper was receding.

"So you sat with your mom. Will you tell me anything about the trip?"

"I can't." He looked away and walked over to my window and peered out, then directly down.

"Seriously? I just don't understand why you won't tell me this stuff. You know I don't go around blabbing your business or anyone else's."

He spun around. "How about you tell me something for a change?" The tone of his voice had turned harsh.

"Huh? I tell you everything."

"Why won't you speak for me?" Zach stood perfectly still. His body became an iceberg.

This time I couldn't bear to look him in the face. "It's not that easy."

"Then I can't answer your questions. Because *it's not that easy* to air our laundry when you're not willing to be with us. That's why."

Those words were daggers to my chest. I swallowed

the lump in my throat and fought back the tears.

I watched him take deep breaths, only to exhale even harder. He ran his hands through his hair, almost looking as if he would grab a handful and yank. Anger was spilling out of him.

I'd be damned if I would cry over this, so I turned toward the wall—not because I was defeated, but rather because he had a point. Nonetheless, I refused to give in because circumstances around us had changed.

Seconds later, his hands came from behind me and slowly slid onto my hips. He breathed over my head, down my hair. Instant comfort. Daggers were pulled from my chest.

"Let's not fight. I'm not perfect, and neither is my family. But I can't spill everything when you won't commit to me. If only you'd speak for—"

"Is that what this boils down to?" I spun around in his arms to face him. My eyes became heavy with tears. "Speaking for you?"

Was I losing him because I wouldn't become a Bertano yet?

His lips turned downward, fighting his own emotional demons. Did he hate that it came down to my favorite subject?

Attempting to comfort me, he took the back of his fingers and softly brushed hair from my eyes. "Yes. I'm sure that's not what you want to hear, but it's the truth. Tatum, if only—"

*Well, isn't this a fine mess I'm in? Nothing like putting the pressure back on.* "If I speak for you, then I won't lose you. Is that what you're saying?"

Zach blinked as his mouth opened, but nothing came out.

"So that's a yes. I don't understand why we just

can't be boyfriend and girlfriend. I'm perfectly committed to you, Zach."

His mouth closed . . . and god help him, he rolled his eyes at me.

"I've never even glanced at another guy, not one. So what's the fucking problem? Why can't they accept—"

A quick moan came from Zach's chest and I met his stare. His eyes drooped. With his arms around my waist, he backed me up against the wall.

The desire for his touch led me to want whatever he did in that moment.

"I accept you, us, exactly the way we are. Right or wrong, my family won't. Or I should say, Gramps won't. But you'll never lose me. I'm yours. Forever. I swear to you, Tatum."

His hands cupped the sides of my face and pulled me closer until my lips were an inch from his. "I want you more than you can imagine." Zach's expression said he had put the diamond on my finger, and then he moved that last inch to my face.

Our lips met with a spark of electricity. My heart was racing a Cheetah for how fast it beat.

If I trusted myself more, I'd have wrapped my legs around his waist and let us fall back onto my bed. Zach overwhelmed me, guaranteeing a chance at a life a girl could only hope for and dream of. We could have it all. Yes! All of our problems would be solved.

I could hear myself breathing. Faster. Faster. Wishing we could be closer, wishing to experience more of him. I placed my arms on his muscular shoulders, taking my hands to the back of his head. Playing with his soft, thick black hair turned me on. So soft. I ran my hands down the sides of his ears. Everything about him was soft and soothing.

That movement seemed to have double meaning, because Zach released my lips and gasped for air. He kissed down my ears, then his lips traveled across my neck.

I wanted him to make me feel this good forever. He trailed kisses down my neckline while he moved his hands to the bottom of my shirt. I never gave Zach the hold-up signal because I wanted him to keep going. I trusted him. He backed away and yanked my sweater over my head.

His eyes expanded while staring at my black lace bra. His chest rose and fell, again and again. Just as mine did.

"Zach?" Not sure why, but I was a bit embarrassed by with him staring at me. He didn't say anything, just stared. The need to cover myself put a damper on my high.

His hand reached for my bra strap and slid it off. "Oh god, Tatum," Zach moaned. He took a breath of air as he brought his head down to my chest.

The anticipation of this new experience sent my head upward, praying I could hold any shrills inside. An electric current zinged down my body as his breath draped my skin.

My breath caught.

Zach froze. Slowly he moved his face to mine and stopped touching me.

I reached up and cupped his cheek. "What's wrong? Why'd you stop?"

His eyes narrowed. Then they squinted, tight. He blinked fast. "I shouldn't have done that to you. I'm sorry."

He turned away and picked my sweater up from the floor, and then handed it to me—not allowing himself another glance at my breasts.

He walked away. Zach looked mad at himself.

I followed him and placed a hand over his shoulder. "Hey . . . you're my boyfriend, and I gave the go-ahead. What's going on?"

He still had his back to me. "If you knew what was going through my mind right now, you wouldn't try to console me." He spun around. The staring began again.

He took his tongue and gently ran it along his perfect lips—Zach looked as if he could rip all of my clothes off. I took a half step back. Not that I didn't want him to touch me, but I feared how far he would take it.

He raised his finger to my face and ran it along my lips. "Touching you . . . you have no idea what I want. I'd give a lot right now for it, too." He looked me right in the eyes. "Hon, I know you don't want to talk about it, but to me . . . you're still a virgin."

My heart skipped a beat, causing me to gasp. A subject that was understandably off-limits. Why would he bring that up? I never loved Kyle, and he definitely didn't love me. Safe to say, Kyle hated me more than anything.

Zach cupped my face. "See . . . I knew how you would react. And I would never take it that far without you fully on board. I want the first time—"

Sex. The subject scared me to death. But . . . with Zach . . . maybe . . . not so scary.

"—we make love to be something you want to give. Something you want more than anything. Your terms. Not up against a wall in your parents' home. You deserve at least that much."

"Oh, Zach." I threw my arms around him and rested my head on his chest. "I love you."

"*Ti amo così tanto,* Tatum."

"I love you so much too, Zach."

We felt great together, natural. No one could be as great as Zach. As great as this. Feeling the connection between us brought tears to my eyes. I never in a million years thought I'd feel such love. My body and soul wanted this, wanted Zach, forever.

"I'm hoping you'll let me know soon if you'll speak for me or not."

I backed away. "How soon?"

"Tomorrow," he answered.

"You know when I make a commitment I keep it. I'm serious . . . I'm not taking this decision lightly. But tomorrow?"

"It's been three weeks, how much more time do you need?" He backed away. "Believe me, things will change when you do. For the better, I promise. I gotta go. And so you know . . ." he glanced around my room, at my windows again. "With everything that's going on, Gramps is wanting to make changes. But you're golden if you speak for me. I'll see you tomorrow."

Of course, Gramps. And just like that, the vision of our perfect world evaporated into thin air. "Sure. I'll talk to you tomorrow."

Zach kissed me goodbye and walked out.

Now I truly knew Gramps controlled everybody. Everything. I had a mom, a controlling mom—I sure as hell didn't need another one. And what did he mean by' I'd be golden'?

## CHAPTER 6

*Tatum*

Hours had gone by since Zach had left, and I wasn't any closer to making a decision when the phone rang. "Hello?"

"Tate? It's Di. Are ya alone?"

"Yeah. What's up?"

"Today. How did things go with Zach? I know he came by your house."

"Confusing. But fine." Until I found out how much she knew, it was vital to tread lightly. Whether I spoke for Zach, or not, I'd honor their privacy.

"I'm just going to say this . . . you know my dad's a St. Louis City cop, right?"

"Of course."

I could hear her huffing. One thing I've learned from being around Zach is if you want information you keep quiet—silence makes most people uncomfortable. Short, direct answers—they get nothing more from you.

"Stop talking like them . . . *Jesus*. Look . . . my dad owed the Bertanos a favor. So, he tipped them off about the feds coming after Sergio."

"Oh . . . thanks for helping?" *Where the hell did that*

*come from? Why did I say that? I mean, of course I'm glad they got a heads-up. Wait. If he's not guilty, then why would they need to prepare?* "Why didn't you tell me this last night?"

"Why are you thanking me? Shit. Don't tell me you spoke for him? Don't tell me it happened already."

"How do you know about that?" I needed to shut my mouth.

Diane exhaled. "I know more than what you do, I'm sure. Now answer me, did you?"

"No. I haven't . . . yet. But you have some explaining to do, missy."

"I didn't know last night. And I'm talking about your relationship with Zach, which is more important. A Bertano is forever, no matter what happens. And the bottom line is, as a friend, a friend that loves you, Tate . . . I'm asking you to be careful. Think this through before it's too late."

*Damn it. It could already be too late.*

She exhaled. "You know I don't get involved for the most part."

"I know."

Her breath came heavier. "But you know how serious this is with him. If Andi was smarter, she'd take her time with Matt, too."

It was no secret Andi and Matt Bertano were falling for each other and fast.

"I don't envy you right now. And whatever you decide, I'll be there," she chuckled. "Like I said last spring, you're gonna always need me."

∞

My bedroom became an asylum for the night. Like

Zach had told me numerous times, "Spoken for, Tate, is our way of committing forever without marriage." For me, the clock was ticking, and the ding for my decision was in final countdown mode.

I wanted to be married, eventually. But to the Mob? It wasn't just Zach alone. I'd be marrying his family too. I didn't want to be another Kate Corleone. Michael had romanced Kate, protected her, and then married her, only to shut her out once she became a wife. Is that how it would be with us? I didn't want to be shut out. But I sure as hell didn't want to participate in their "politics," either. And why would I assume real life was like a movie? But it would be like a movie. Wouldn't it?

But the fricking Mob? A fricking Mob movie?

No. I didn't want that at all.

I slipped on my pink Holly Hobbie jammies and examined myself in the floor mirror.

"Seriously," I said out loud. "You a Mobster's girlfriend? A Mob wife? Shit." I chuckled in a huff. "This is insane."

I was nothing like the Italian women I knew. I had blond hair with pale skin, a look that would fit perfectly with ribbons tied around pigtails and Dutch wooden shoes. A white apron around my waist. So, why me?

The mirror was no help at all. I slipped on my robe and walked into the living room. Mom and Dad were watching the news. I glanced over, making sure the Bertanos weren't on the TV again. All clear.

I sat with Mom on the couch. "Sorry, but I need to talk."

I'd hit rock bottom. I never before wanted my dad's advice and help, let alone my mother's.

My mother jerked her head at me. "About what?"

"Nothing bad, just about college."

She let her shoulders drop. "Oh, okay."

"I was wondering if you think I'll be able to go? I'm sure I'll get some scholarships, but not a full ride. Will there be enough money?"

Dad excitedly said, "Sure. We were going to tell you this Christmas that your grandmother left you a college fund. We can talk about it now, though. Are you thinking about schools to apply to?"

"Not yet, Dad, but soon."

"You should be fine," Dad said. "But so you know, Granny left you money for college tuition. Nothing else, Tate."

"Really? Great. I just wanted to make sure about money before I made any plans."

"What kind of plans?" Mother had one eyebrow cocked.

"College, Mom. Why do you always assume something else?" *Like marrying the Mob!*

She turned toward Dad. I caught him slowly shaking his head at her. "She doesn't, Tate. Look, if there's one thing Grandma did for you, she set you up to be very independent. I'm just glad to hear you're thinking about your future already. You had me worried that you and Zach were getting . . . a little . . . too close. You need to go to college, Tate."

Bingo.

"I agree. Thanks, Dad. I'm going to bed now. Work in the morning." A sore subject between my mother and me. She made me take a job for "play money"—that's how she referred to my losing my weekends.

"'Night," they both said.

An hour went by with me staring up at the dark ceiling. I couldn't sleep or come to a decision. Every time my mind took Zach out of my future, I immediately felt sick. Clammy sweats. Depressed all over again. A gut feeling that I would not be able to go on without him.

This was life-changing. I had to be smart about everything. Some girls might run to the thrill of the Mob. Not me. Zach's direction was where I'd run. Right into his arms.

It didn't help, either, that every time I closed my eyes, he was there in my head.

Minutes later, I found myself in a sweat, thinking about the kisses he gave me, the hugs, the love and protection.

I wiped my forehead with the back of my hand.

Zach was everything I'd hoped for in a guy, but for one enormous factor that couldn't be changed. *Can I live with the Mob forever? How am I supposed to know?* The more I thought about the situation, the less I wanted to know. I curled up in the covers with Gizmo. The terrier was a great cuddler.

My body relaxed again. Sleep. I needed some sleep.

*Grandma's blue eyes sparkled like I remembered. We stood in total blackness, nothing and nobody around but for Grandma and me.*

*She took my hand in hers. I felt the veins road-mapped on her hand. The veins I used to press on when I was younger, fascinated by how they moved.*

*"Well, Grandma, I've tried. Just like you taught me. But evidently, I can't read guys worth a crap. Like with Kyle—that was a disaster. Then I knew there was something different about Zach, and yet I couldn't see*

*his dark side. What makes me think I'm reading him right?"*

*"What do you think you see?"*

*"Secrets. Danger. Obligations that follow him. On the flip side, I see someone who's sincere and loyal. He loves me, Grandma. All traits I shouldn't turn away from. Don't we all have obligations?"*

*"True, we all do, but you're right, Zach's are more serious. That said, you would need to look past them. Why do you feel you can't live without him, though?"*

*"I can, I just don't know if I want to."*

*"Can you live with everything his life brings into yours?"*

*"I don't know. I'm scared."*

*"If you have any reservations, you shouldn't be involved with that family, Tatey. Fear is not love. They eat fear for a snack."*

*"So you think I shouldn't speak for him?"*

*"Not for me to say. Just remember his hand means forever. What about college? What have you always said about getting away? The Bertanos won't allow you to be independent the way you've dreamt of."*

*"But, Grandma, every time I think about not being with him forever, I can't imagine us apart. For some strange reason, I feel as if he'll always be there for me."*

*"So, you do love him?"*

*"I do. But not his family."*

*"Package deal."*

*"I know."*

*"I trust you, Tatey. Whatever you decide, I'll always be here for you. Always."*

Beep. Beep. Beep. My alarm was screaming.

## CHAPTER 7

*Tatum*

Time was against me. I had to talk to Zach before work. In the bathroom, I hurriedly applied makeup and tossed my uniform on a hanger. I darted for my phone in the bedroom, closed the door, and dialed Zach's mobile. Once I'd made up my mind, I had to get it over with. Wouldn't drag this out, nor keep Zach hanging.

"Hello?" Zach picked up on the first ring.

The second I heard his voice, my decision wavered. My heart sank. That attractive voice made me debate if this was the wrong call or not. "Hi, Zach, it's Tate—"

"What's wrong? Are you okay? Did he get in your window?"

"What? No. I'm fine. What are you talking about?"

"Nothing. Go on."

"I wanted to see if we could chat before I go to work. I won't keep you."

"Of course. Can you come here, or do you want me to come to your house?"

"Not here. My family is still home. Let me stop by real fast."

His voice sounded clipped. "Come to Tyler's. We're in back, at the pool."

My chest heaved. Just a bit longer and it would be over with.

With no time to waste, I jogged to the kitchen, where my family was having breakfast.

"Mom, Dad . . . would you guys mind if I run an errand before going to work? I won't be long," I said, out of breath from hurrying.

Dad shrugged. "Sure." He shoved a bite of hash browns in his mouth. He looked up at me and cringed. "Dear Lord, Tatum. Why are your eyes bloodshot?"

That got my mother's attention. She tried to examine my face. "Have you been crying?"

My hand went up to my forehead to try to cover my haggardness. "I didn't sleep. It's no big deal. I need to get Visine before work. I'm just nervous about this new job."

Dad went back to eating. "Don't be late, and come straight home afterward."

Mom swayed her head to the side. "Well, hurry up. I don't want you looking like that. And be careful with my car."

"I won't be late. Thanks." I ran out the door.

I hung up my uniform in the backseat and noticed I was working up to have a heart attack. My chest was killing me. At the stoplight, I glanced in the rearview mirror, only to have a hot mess looking back at me: my swollen eyes had dark circles underneath and the whites were red. "Just breathe, Tate. Zach's always said it's my choice. He would never force me to do anything." *Sure, he says that now, but would that change?*

The light turned green. Crap, why couldn't I just stay stuck at a red light forever?

The whole time I drove to the Bertano house, my hands shook. Surprisingly, I kept the car on the road. Minutes later, I was pulling into their neighborhood. Turning down a street, my hands were slipping on the steering wheel from so much sweat. One by one, I wiped them off on the side of my legs. Trying to scold myself into calming down didn't work.

I pulled in their drive and sat for a minute, staring up at the "normal" house, but there was nothing normal about them.

"Dear Lord, I hope you know what you're doing," I said to myself. One last look in the mirror, but what was the point? No amount of makeup could camouflage a long night of crying. I looked like death warmed over twice, resurrected, and then killed again. I took my sleeve and dabbed at the corners of my eyes.

I went up to their front door and knocked.

I had to get this over with.

Tyler greeted me. "Tatum. Come in, I'll show you to the pool house."

I'll be damned . . . the same Bertano smirk spread across Tyler's face. *How is that? Do they imprint that smirk in the genes or something?* "Thanks."

He escorted me through the house.

I assumed Zach had told him to expect me. In the back of the house, Tyler stepped through a wall of glass doors and out into the backyard. It was an image straight out of a *Better Homes and Gardens* magazine, with a half-glass pool house on the right side.

Tyler escorted me through a doorway and toward the inground pool.

Zach was walking toward me with a towel around his shoulders. "Saw you coming."

Matt was reclining on the edge of the pool, holding a

beer. Tyler paused and gave him a long stare. Bobby walked in a back door, looking as if he'd just run a few miles. Zach glanced at him, making eye contact before Bobby nodded at him.

"I thought we'd be alone," I murmured.

Zach took his hand through his black hair, grinning at me. I tried not to stare at what I'd be missing out on, but what girl wouldn't peek at a handsome guy in front of her? A rock-hard body with water caressing his tanned skin. Damn it.

*Do not watch him. He'll make you think his way is the right way. Be strong. Plant those feet. Sexy or not, you must. It's the right thing to do.*

"Tate, you all right? You look tense," Zach said.

"I just need to talk to you." My breaths were uneven.

I couldn't take much more. Zach made the simple act of drying off incredibly sexy. He bent to dry his legs. He stood and wrapped the towel around his waist.

"We'll go in the back for some privacy." Zach put his hand out for me.

I wished he hadn't done that. He noticed the sweat.

He glanced back at me. His eyes widened in surprise. That did it—he knew.

*Don't cry yet. Not yet. Just wait till you leave. Please, Tatum, do not let him see you cry. It'll be all right.*

Zach turned his back to me.

I stopped dead in my tracks.

Bam . . . a blazing bold tattoo in the middle of Zach's shoulder blades stared back at me. Inked in black were interlocking fingers, gripped in a bond. Above the interlocking hands, Bertano was spelled out in blood red.

The enormous tattoo moved with Zach's muscles as

he walked. That was one of the largest tattoos I'd ever seen. A gasp of air escaped from between my lips.

Zach stopped mid-step, but didn't turn back to me. "We're to proudly wear our family's sign once we turn sixteen, no matter what. The men must have them." He continued taking me down the hall. "All of my sons will get the same when they turn sixteen."

I tried to pull my hand away, but his grip tightened.

We stopped at the last door down the hall. Zach dropped my hand. He stood off to the side of the doorway and waved. "In here."

I went inside a small changing room with a bench seat and a mirror. I took the bench. Zach shut the door and locked it. If only my heart would let me get this out before I keeled over.

Leaning up against the doorway, he crossed his arms.

Oh he knew, all right. And he'd locked me in here. He had to know what was coming. He wasn't smiling. His eyebrows drew together and his eyes pierced mine.

*Tate, just breathe.*

Hands fiddling in my lap . . . "I love you." I looked up at his eyes. "I mean it."

"I love you too, Tatum." Zach's face changed, his eyes softened.

I couldn't look at him without crying. "I know you do. That's why this is so hard for me—"

"Say what you have to say, Tate." Zach's voice was ice-cold.

I was afraid to make eye contact with him again, but I did. "I don't love everything."

"Are you telling me you won't commit because of my family? Is that what this is about? You're not speaking for me?"

I leaped to my feet. "No." I touched his crossed arms. "I love who you are, Zach. I don't love your family enough to be involved like that. I'm not committing—"

"Tate, I am my family. You either want to be with me or you don't. A package deal."

The exact same thing Grandma had said last night, *package deal*.

My heart was breaking. "If that's how it's going to be, Zach, then my answer is no." I took a step back, hoping it would be easier to look away, because deep down I was reconsidering my decision. Hurting him was the last thing I wanted to do.

"You know what, you can say no. It won't matter anyway."

"What?" I snapped, jerking my head back toward him.

He uncrossed his arms. His posture relaxed. "Did you honestly think your decision would change mine?"

Where was this coming from? He sounded mad. No, he sounded crazy.

"Don't look at me as if you had no idea. Come on, Tate. You said yourself how this isn't something to take lightly, and I haven't. I *mean* my commitment. Don't speak for me, but you're spoken for. I'll rot in hell before I change that."

"Uh, I gotta go to work. I'm sorry, Zach. It's just . . ." I went to cup the side of his face like he had mine so many times before.

He jerked away, rejecting me. Zach was pissed. I never wanted him mad at me.

I bit on my bottom lip. "I'm sorry." I choked down a sob. My goal of trying not to cry in front of him was a failure.

Without thinking, I reached for the door handle. He backed away to let me run out. The moment he moved, I flung the door open with such force it vibrated on impact. Zach turned to the side and put his fist through the drywall. The sound of ripping flesh and caving sheet rock had me biting my tongue.

I ran down the hall with my hands covering my face.

Our time together flashed through my mind—Zach's kisses—his arms—his warmth . . . his love.

I was running away from it all.

*This better be the right decision, because it's fucking killing me.*

I refrained from screaming. To avoid collapsing to my knees, I ran my hand along the wall for strength. I was trying to get to my car.

I never wanted to fall in love again.

*This hurts. Hurts way . . . way too much.*

"Go! Walk away. But damn it, Tatum Frances Duncan, this isn't over," Zach yelled from behind me. "I'll love you. Forever."

# CHAPTER 8

### Zach

Once Tatum ran out the pool house door and headed for her car, Gramps's world collapsed on my chest. She'd left me. I kept trying to convince myself otherwise, but there wasn't a rational factor that said she hadn't. No. She'd left me. She hadn't just left—she'd run away.

Matt got out of the pool and dried off.

Bobby walked toward me.

I couldn't look either one in the eye.

Adding insult to injury, Tyler came in the pool house from the door Tatum had run out of seconds earlier. Great, here came the cavalry, telling me what I already knew—I was screwed.

"Well, that complicates things," Tyler said.

"No shit, Captain Obvious." I turned away from all of them. "Why? Why would she leave it all? You know this is all Kyle's fault. All because that fuck-head won't leave her the hell alone, I went to Gramps. Then I find out the old man is talking about me and Mariacella getting hitched or something. Telling me there's other fish in the fucking sea."

"You're shitting me?" Bobby laughed.

I turned to face him. "No."

Bobby looked at Matt, their snickering gone. Tyler didn't budge.

I focused my attention back to him. "So let me guess . . . you knew Gramps has been talking to Davide?"

"Yes. Well, just found out. We were told after you and Cat left his office yesterday. Sorry, but you need to announce Tatum's decision to leave you. Today. I feel for you. We all swore she wouldn't walk."

"Yeah, well, she did." I dropped my forehead against the wall. "I shouldn't have pushed her. I thought if she'd just speak for me, Gramps would assign some security. And I was right to worry. She said her dog must have ripped her screen, but I wasn't fooled. Her screen was cut. I guess she had her window locked, so he gave up."

"Zach?" Bobby said. "I'm sorry. I didn't watch him the night the police came. I said I would and I didn't."

I lifted my forehead from the wall and faced them. "Bob, don't. It's the way things happen . . . all at fucking once. Sergio was life or death."

They all looked at each other.

I took a deep breath. "Sergio was immediate. You know what I mean. Let it go. Matt, do you think Andi would spend more time with Tate on the weekends? Just so she's not alone so much."

The big guy took a seat at the patio table next to me. "Of course. But what are you going to do?"

"Besides slitting my wrists . . . I guess go back to Gramps and tell him. I can't push Tate anymore . . . look what good it did this time."

Later that afternoon, Tyler drove me out to the Hill.

He parked in back, the same spot I'd used the day

before.

"Can I offer you some advice, Zach?"

"Don't say, *Hold your temper*." I rolled my eyes at him.

Tyler shoved the shifter into park and angled himself to face me. "No, smart-ass . . . I was going to say, he won't want to listen right now with Sergio's mess—"

"You mean our mess? If one goes down, we *all* go down."

"Of course. Listen . . . I heard Gramps and Davide really like the idea of our families combining. They're getting hard-ons thinking about the money and enterprise they could pull together. No matter what, tell Gramps you intend to stay spoken for Tate. Screw everything else right now."

He was right. I needed to stay focused on remaining Tate's. I would deal with the Mariacella issue later. Hopefully much later.

When we stood in the doorway of Gramps's office, he waved Tyler and me in.

Gramps was on the phone, so we shut the door behind us. He pointed for us to take seats in front of his desk. He did this every time someone came to talk to him. I figured I'd take the chair my mother had sat in last time, since the other one hadn't given me any luck.

"And you're getting Sergio, then coming here, Nicola?" Gramps said into the phone.

He was talking with my dad. I couldn't wait for him to return. Mom didn't sleep last night with him in Switzerland.

"*Grazie*, Nicola. You have made me very happy, my son. Now, back here your Zacharia has been busy."

Great. Now he'll worry Dad.

Gramps grinned at me, puffing away on his stogie.

"*Ragazza* problems." Gramps laughed. "Yeah, the good kind of *problema*. See you soon, *arrivederci*." Gramps placed the phone on the receiver. "Zacharia, what happened so soon?"

I took a long, purposeful breath and gently exhaled to calm my nerves. "Gramps, hear me out first."

He chuckled. "Don't I always?"

Yeah, that was funny. "Yes, sir. I want to stay spoken for Tate. But today she called things off with me."

He puffed. "What's this you say? Called what off? She hasn't spoken for you."

"That's right, she hasn't. And now she may not. She broke up with me."

Gramps sat back in his leather chair and turned away, examining the ceiling. "Let me get this straight . . . she's broken up with you." He looked at me. "It's over?"

I nodded.

He turned away again. "And yet, you want her to remain spoken for by you? Why?"

This was exhausting. "Simple. I rushed her. Last night, I told her to give me a decision today. She freaked and ran. It's my fault. I want to give her more time, because I believe she'll reconsider."

"So, it goes back to giving this girl time. Listen to me, Zacharia." He leaned forward, placing his forearms on the edge of his desk. "I won't bullshit you . . . I'm tired of this girl already—"

There was a call on my mobile.

Gramps nodded for me to see who was calling. Tyler glanced over at me.

I looked down at the caller ID. It was Tatum. What did she want? Judging by the time, she had probably just gotten off work. "It's her." I kept my voice smooth . . . smooth as her hair. I powered the mobile off.

Gramps chair squeaked as he reclined. "You can answer her later. Nothing will change this now."

"What do you mean? Nothing will change what now?" Had he already made his damn decision? Shit.

"Sir, if I may?" Tyler spoke up.

"Yes, *Primo*. What's your take on this Tatum he's so damn fond of?"

Tyler paused. I glanced over at him, secretly begging him to cut me some slack. He didn't blink, completely ignored me.

"I would agree with letting Zach stay spoken for her." Tyler brought his hand up. "I know the rule, and this disobeys it, but she is loyal, like Cat has said. And she does seem to love Zach. Unfortunately, Tate's been through a few things recently."

Now I owed Tyler, damn it. Worth it, though.

Gramps puffed. Not saying a word, but taking his sweet time evaluating each of us. The damn Italian stubbornness that coursed my veins came directly from that man.

Gramps let out a huge ball of smoke. "All right. You want to stay committed to this German girl, then fine, here's the deal." He nodded his fat cigar at us. "You keep her in. But if you don't get her to change her mind before we leave for Italy in three weeks, all bets are off. You rescind your commitment or I keep you in Italy with Vito."

"You're saying if Tate doesn't commit by the time we leave for Italy, and I don't rescind, I'm being forced to *live in Italy*?"

Pounding his fist on the desk, Gramps leaned forward. "Yes. You put me in a tough spot, I'll put you in a tough spot. Why can't you understand how much I dislike you committing to a girl who has rejected us? This Tatum does not understand us."

*Damn it. I do understand his view. He's right, but why can't he see how much she means to me?*

I sat back. No use fighting him. I'd gotten what I wanted, more time.

Gramps's phone rang, and he snatched it off the receiver. "*Siediti*," Gramps yelled.

He looked up and shoed us with his hand, dismissing us. "*Un minuto*," he said. Gramps pulled the phone away from his face. "Three weeks, Zacharia. She has three weeks."

Tyler closed the door behind us. "*Jesus*. Gramps can't pronounce Tatum's name at all." He laughed.

I thudded my back against the wall, thanking god Gramps gave me at least a few weeks. No screwing around. I'd do whatever it would take to get Tate to change her mind. I'd known this would happen. I should have never demanded a decision today. This was my fault.

Noise from the restaurant distracted me.

I looked up. My dad, Uncle Piero, and Uncle Sergio had walked in the family's private entrance. If it were my mother standing there, she would have come running for me, but this was my dad and he didn't run for anybody.

Tyler stepped next to me. "Nicola doesn't look happy. Sergio does, though."

We both knew Sergio was getting out of legal trouble and Dad had done something he didn't want to. Always for the benefit of the family.

Dad stepped up to me and patted my shoulder. "Zach, Mother told me what's been going on. You okay?"

I nodded. "Sergio, Piero."

They nodded back and then stepped into the employee lounge without a word. We followed. It was tight in there with Matt's dad, Uncle Piero—he was called Monster for a reason. Tyler made sure we were alone, looking under the stalls.

Piero stood at the door, leaning up against the wall. Tyler and Sergio sat on the sofa in the sitting area.

Dad stood before me. "What just happened in there? What did he say?"

"Until we leave for the holidays in three weeks—that's all the time I have to get Tatum back and to make her speak for me."

Dad's eyebrows shot up. "She broke up with you? Like . . . not just rejected us, but you?"

*Damn it . . . now to drop the bomb on Dad.*

"Zach gave her an ultimatum last night because of the whole Kyle security thing. Zach asked for her commitment ASAP," Tyler said.

Dad spun around, throwing his hands up in the air.

Exactly what I felt like doing.

Dad turned back to face me again. "This all took place in twenty-four hours?"

I nodded. "Less."

Dad rubbed his forehead. "Son, you have the timing of a cereal box watch."

My dad's eyes were red. Not sure if I had ever seen him this tired. "You okay, Dad?"

He exhaled and grinned. "Sure, son." He placed his hand on my shoulder. "But what I want you to do now is go to her. Do whatever it takes to get Tate back. Worry about her speaking for you later. Don't even mention it to her this week."

Sergio got up from the couch and walked up to us. "I owe you and your father."

"No, you don't." Dad waved his hand.

"Yeah, I do. Zach, what can I do? And this will remain between us. I swear."

Within seconds, it was settled. I was getting security for Tatum. Not sure if I was happy or not about going behind Gramps's back. But since I had two Leads—my dad and Tyler—backing this up, why argue?

## CHAPTER 9

*Tatum*

Starting my weekend off by telling Zach that I would not be "speaking for" him was not ideal. Zach warned me as I ran out of his house, not able to face him a moment longer—"Damn it, Tatum Frances Duncan, this isn't over . . . I'll love you. Forever."

This wasn't over? What did he mean by that? Because before I broke up with him, he called me five times a day, or he would show up at my house. Now, nothing.

Accepting no contact from him was a tough pill to swallow. Right or wrong, I wanted to remain friends—famous last words. But true. We were friends first, and once I'd fallen in love with him, my biggest fear had been that if things went south, we wouldn't remain friends. But no, he'd persisted, saying I'd never lose him no matter what happened. He'd lied.

If only he'd answer his damn phone, he could tell me to bug off. I'd called him numerous times, and now it was going straight to voicemail. He must have shut it off.

To make sure, I tried again.

His mobile went straight to voicemail.

"This is Zach Bertano. Leave your message after the beep." A long beep followed and then a click.

"Uh . . . Zach, hi. It's me . . . Tate. Yes, I'm trying you again. It's after seven. Would you mind calling me? I'd like to see you. Um. Okay. Talk to ya later."

An hour later, I still hadn't heard from Zach. My house was winding down for the night, but I wasn't. I lay on my bed, staring up at the ceiling, thinking about him. He said my bed made him feel seasick. Silly boy! Everything reminded me of Zach.

I missed him. Why was he avoiding me? He'd said it wasn't over. And I believed him.

The picture of us at homecoming sat on my nightstand. The frame he'd bought for the photo was an antique—beautifully decorated in brushed ornate steel, twisted and curved. Kind of like our relationship.

I held it up, examining us in that moment. We both looked so happy and in love.

Did it mean nothing?

Not possible.

But Zach not calling me, not even to say *go take a hike,* sent a clear message. The message: *You broke up with me. It's over.*

He had every right to say that, too.

Whether he had every right to ignore me or not, the constant reminders of him drove me crazy. I walked down to my dad's workshop in the basement and brought up an empty box to my room. I collected everything that shouted *Zach* and tossed it in the box, down to the strapless bra I'd bought specifically for the homecoming dress. The damn dress he couldn't bear to see me in without reacting. The dress he'd unzipped while kissing my neck. I could feel the kisses all over again as if it were happening. Down my shoulders, soft kisses continued all over my bare skin. Until I stopped him at the lacy strapless bra. This bra.

Maybe it would be easier for me if things went back to the way they'd been before the kiss. The kiss we'd had when we were becoming more than just friends. The *amazing* kiss that had now led to pain.

The thought of the insane experience against my wall the night before, and looking at the lace bra, made my heart sink like the *Titanic*. I wanted to feel that rush again, the rush you get when you know you're loved. He made me feel that way. Every day I felt more love from him than I ever had.

Why wouldn't he answer my calls?

Just a simple fricking phone call. If he was intentionally giving me the silent treatment and trying to drive me mad, then by god he'd achieved his goal.

Not able to take the silence, I held the bra up to my face and screamed. *How could he? It can't be over. I won't accept it was all or nothing. He said it—he said it wasn't over. So why? In his car at homecoming, he said I'd never lose him. Even as just friends. So WHY?*

I frantically picked up my phone and dialed his mobile again. The same damn recording and beeps. I took a deep breath. "Fine. Don't talk to me. But I still love—" The ugly cry came gushing out of me. "You." I hiccupped. I held my breath to slow my breathing and sniffled. "You said it wasn't over. But then you don't talk to me. So fuck you."

I stabbed our lifeline through the heart, killing us further with my anger.

"No." I panicked. *Don't piss him off more.* "I'm sorry. I'm . . . I'm sorry. Just please don't let this be it.

Can't we take this slow? Please?" I sniffled. Crying so hard I could barely talk, and if I wasn't pathetic enough, my nose wouldn't stop running. "Sorry. Just . . . let's talk. Please?" I slammed the phone down on the receiver, hoping to god I'd made the right decision by not speaking for him.

I caught the end of a made-for-TV movie, I worked up enough energy to look at the nightstand. There sat the silent phone, and the ache in my chest began again. How pathetic . . . eight thirty on a Saturday evening and I was already in bed. I wanted to give him one last call for the night, then I'd give up. I dialed, faster than I could come up with one good reason not to call.

His voice came on with the instructions for leaving a message. Just hearing him made my chest heave.

*God . . . I miss him so bad and it's only been nine hours.*

The beep . . .

"Um, Zach. Yeah, it's me. I miss you." I took a deep breath. Took another breath—"Not sure what's going on, but I'm assuming this is a solid message. You're cutting me off. I understand. I do. So, I guess I'll see ya in school." It took every bit of willpower I had to hang up. I even had to use my other hand to force the phone down on the receiver.

∞

I must have fallen asleep, because once the phone rang, I almost fell off the bed. No matter how disoriented I was, I jerked the phone from the receiver. "Hello?"

"Hey, Tate! It's Val."

I hadn't talked to my childhood friend for weeks.

We'd grown up together since our parents had lived across the hall from each other in the same apartment complex. I trusted her with anything. Outside of Zach and his cousins, she was the only one who knew what Kyle did to me.

"Oh, hey." I sat up, glancing over at the nightstand clock. Almost nine o'clock.

"You sound tired. You okay?"

"I dozed off." My breath caught and I sniffled.

"Have you been crying?"

*Here we go . . .* "Yeah . . . Zach and I broke up." Hearing those words come out of my mouth pissed me off. This was stupid. Zach and I should be together. How could I let one old man ruin what I wanted so badly?

She gasped. "No!"

"I can't talk about it right now. I've been crying all night as it is."

"I understand. Scotty and I will pick you up in twenty minutes. Be ready."

"No thanks, I'm not—"

"Not an option. See ya soon."

Click.

Not sure why I looked at the phone, but I did. "Hello? Val?" She'd hung up on me.

I jumped out of bed and threw clothes on, knowing her well enough to recognize she wasn't bluffing. What sucked was that I wanted company—just not her boyfriend's company.

"Mom," I called down the hall. "Is it okay if I go out with Val and her boyfriend for a bit?" Putting my jeans on and talking seemed too much for me to do at once. I hopped around, trying to avoid falling down face-first.

Mom stormed into my bedroom. "I thought you

were in bed?"

"Was, until she called. Didn't you hear the phone?"

"No, we were outside talking to the neighbor."

"Well, is it okay?"

"I suppose, for a bit." She crossed her arms and leaned against the corner of my wall. "Zach with his family tonight?"

No way in hell was I telling her about our break-up. I had to take a deep breath to avoid tears. *If only Zach was picking me up . . . nope, this is what I deserve. I did this to us. What did I think would happen?* "Yeah, he's with them."

Her chin lowered, and she looked right through me. I didn't give her the satisfaction. Not to mention I did have to hurry to get dressed and freshen up. I ran to the bathroom. "Gotta brush my teeth. We won't be late. Promise."

I closed the bathroom door and braced my hands on the sink, looking in the mirror at myself. "Idiot. She knows you broke up with him. But she thinks it's because of his uncle."

I shook my head in hopes it'd release disgust within myself, but it didn't. *Wish Scotty wasn't going to be with Val. Damn it, I'd like a girlfriend tonight. I need one. We could curl up in my bed, watching sappy movies, eating a bucket of popcorn, and washing it down with Dove chocolates. I should have called Di. She knows the Bertanos and would understand.*

"Tate? A car just pulled up," Mom called.

I ran out of the bathroom and to my bedroom, pulling a sweatshirt over my head.

"Tate?" Mom walked into my bedroom. "It's not Scott's car."

I shoved my blinds out of the way and looked

outside. It wasn't Scotty's car. It was a big cream-colored Mercedes. Resembled a Bertano car because of the tinted windows. Could it be his mom or dad? My heart skipped a beat, praying it was. Sad how eager I was to meet them now.

Then Val got out of the back seat and ran up to the door. I jerked back, dropping the blinds. "Val's running up."

The doorbell chimed.

"I'll go let her in," Mom said.

A moment later, Val walked in my room with the brightest smile on her face. "I told you twenty minutes."

"Yeah. Yeah. Yeah." I grabbed my purse. "I thought you said you and Scotty were picking me up?"

"We are. Let's go." Val walked out of my room. "See ya in a few hours, Mr. and Mrs. Duncan." Val waved bye to them as we exited the living room.

Of course Mom had to reiterate my curfew.

For some unknown reason, when I slammed the front door shut behind me, my life felt different. Weird. Maybe it was simply leaving with Val instead of Zach.

Val opened the back door of the car, but I was confused why she didn't go for the front with Scotty. I struggled to see past the tinted windows. Scotty was in back, and Val jumped in next to him.

Val turned back to me. "What are you doing?"

Wasn't it obvious what I was doing? I ducked to see inside the huge Mercedes, and in the driver's seat was the guy we'd run into at the mall last summer. The British guy who resembled a dark-haired James Dean. The guy I couldn't stand to face because he was so fricking cute.

He looked back at me, leaning his forearm over the

passenger seat. My heart sank.

*Valerie . . . you didn't*, was all I could think. No. No way in hell was I entertaining this pathetic scheme of hers.

Mr. British James Dean grinned at me. "Hop in."

I hopped in all right. Straight in the back seat.

I shoved Val over and quickly closed the door before anyone could say differently. I stared out the window, thinking about Zach. Looking at my front door, where just the day before he'd given me a goodbye kiss. Our last kiss. I wanted to be with him. He'd kill me if he knew I hopped in a car with another guy. No matter what Zach might have thought, *I didn't want this at all.*

I reached for the door handle, but it was too late, the car drove off. Too slow on the draw. Val was giving me the what-is-your-fucking-problem face. I forced down the lump in my throat.

## CHAPTER 10

### Zach

I headed straight for Tatum's house, praying her parents wouldn't get mad at me for knocking on her door at nine thirty.

I'd turned my mobile back on when Tyler drove me to get my car, and saw that Tate had called four times. I'd never heard her sound so pitiful and weak.

This could be her wanting to reconsider her decision. I could have Tate back tonight.

In front of her house, I got out of the car as fast as I could. Tatum's bedroom was pitch black inside. My pulse sped up seventeen more notches. *Something's wrong.*

I ran up to the door and knocked, it opened.

"Hello, Mrs. Duncan. I hope it's not too late to be here, but is Tate home?"

She swallowed so loudly I thought she'd choke. "Oh . . . I'm sorry, Zach. She just left."

I didn't think it was possible for her to act any weirder than she normally did, but she proved me wrong. "Uh . . . okay. I kind of need to talk to her. Do you know if she's coming back soon?" I didn't want to come out and ask where the hell Tate went, but I was getting close.

"I'm sorry, Zach. She left with a girlfriend. I don't think she'll be back till curfew. I can tell her you came by."

"Sorry for twenty questions, but is she out with Diane?"

"No. She left with Val."

"Cynthia, what's going on?" Tatum's dad called.

"Ken, it's Zach."

Mr. Duncan walked up and opened the screen door, leaning his shoulder against the frame. "How are you, kid?"

Mrs. Duncan backed away and whispered too loudly, "You take care of this."

"Look, Mr. Duncan, I don't mean to cause any problems—"

"Oh, don't worry." Mr. Duncan waved his hand. "But Tate's not home. You just missed her. She left about five minutes ago. Went out with her old girlfriend, Val. Is this important?"

*Important to me, yeah.* "It's complicated, sir. Do you know if she's working tomorrow morning?"

"She is, till five."

"Thanks. I'll talk to her later then, 'night."

"Sure thing. We'll let her know you came by." Her dad closed the door.

*Damn it to hell. She's talked about this to Val, but I have no clue where they could be.*

Back in my car, I got my phone out.

Bobby answered on the first ring. "Yeah, Zach?"

"Hey, Tate's not home, she's supposedly out with her childhood friend, Val. What time did you say you'll be at her house?"

"Whenever, but the later the better. Best to make sure all the neighbors are in bed."

"Tate has to be home by eleven. Meet me here at two."

"Sure. What are you going to do? Wait for her?"

"Yeah. I don't want her parents to see me out here. I'm going to get something to eat and then park down the street. That way I'll be here when Tate gets dropped off."

## CHAPTER 11

*Tatum*

Thank god looks can't kill.

"What the hell, Tate? Why didn't you get in front with Nigel?" Val whispered through gritted teeth.

*Good, she said his name, I'd forgotten it. Of course I forgot . . . I haven't put another thought toward him, since I'm in love with Zach. Damn it, Val.*

To avoid further embarrassment, I kept my voice low. "What did I tell you, like . . . oh, I don't know . . . half an hour ago? You honestly think I'm going to entertain this idea of yours? You're sick."

"Uh, Mate . . . shall I still go to Denny's?" The British guy, Nigel, asked.

I didn't know what was going on, but I wasn't sure this Nigel did either.

Scotty looked over at Val and me, rolling his eyes. "Yeah, Nigel. Thanks."

Nigel glanced in the rearview mirror. Our eyes met in the dark, but he quickly dropped his stare. Not that I owed this guy anything, but I didn't want to hurt his feelings either. He could be an innocent bystander like me.

Minutes later, we pulled into Denny's. Scotty opened his door, and Val jumped out behind him, slamming their door behind her, leaving me. I sat there, not sure what to do. It would be a long walk home.

Val and Scotty were walking into Denny's. Nigel got out of the car and walked across the front of the Mercedes, heading toward my car door. This wasn't how I'd planned to spend my evening. Damn it.

Nigel opened the door and looked down at me.

His expression was soft. "Hi. Um, we met a while back at the mall. I'm Nigel." He put his hand out.

I'd kill Val later, after I was nice to this guy. It wouldn't be right to take my anger toward Val out on him.

I accepted his handshake. "I'm Tatum." I got out of the car and stepped aside.

He gently closed the door and faced me with a knockout smile. "Not sure what those two idiots had in mind, but I get the feeling they hoped to set us up."

After listening to his British accent, I suddenly missed Zach's Italian accent.

Out of the corner of my eye, I caught Val and Scotty being seated against the window in a corner booth. I let out a frustrated sigh. "I'm positive that's what they wanted."

Nigel glanced over at Denny's and then down at his biker boots.

"I'm going to be honest, Nigel." He looked up at me. Damn. He had the bluest eyes, and eyelashes thicker than Marilyn Monroe's. Eyelashes a girl would kill for. "Today I kind of—" I had to breathe, feeling the panic the next words brought to me. "Broke up with my boyfriend."

Nigel took half a step back. "I didn't know."

"Yeah, so knowing what those idiots are attempting, I wouldn't feel right not telling you up front. I'm sorry, I just can't do this."

He glanced over at the restaurant again, and back at me with a grin. "Thanks for telling me, because my mates neglected to mention any of that."

Nigel scanned the area, shoving his hands in his back pockets, forcing his black t-shirt to stretch over his chest.

I'd never seen anyone so unsure of asking me something as this guy was.

"I am hungry. Would you mind coming in so I can eat first, and then I promise to drive you home? No hard feelings."

"Of course not, this isn't your fault. Let's go."

He turned to the side and put his hand out, signaling for me to walk ahead of him.

Not only did Val and Scotty sucker me into this idea of theirs without any warning, it appeared they'd done the same to Nigel. Those two really needed to get a life and leave everyone else's alone.

Nigel grabbed the door and opened it for me. He smiled.

With Nigel behind me, we stepped up to the half-moon booth. I forced Val to scoot in and Nigel did the same on Scotty's side. I wasn't worried about giving Val the look of death because what caught my attention was Nigel's look to Scotty.

"You're a wanker," Nigel mumbled under his breath.

That said it all. Whether I was interested or not, and I wasn't, Nigel could give one hell of an *I'm pissed at you* look, and Scotty was on the receiving end. They deserved it. Maybe it was confirmation Nigel didn't know I was with Zach. And that made Nigel cool with me.

Our booth remained silent during dinner, but it was clear Val and Scotty were getting the message loud and clear.

Val finished her salad and scooted toward me. "Let's go to the bathroom."

I slid out of the booth without responding and followed her to the ladies' room.

Once the door closed I spun around, braced myself on the counter and confronted Val.

She wouldn't face me. "Okay, so you're mad. I get that. But something told me to call you tonight. To see if you'd go out with us." Val had the nerve to give me puppy dog eyes. "How could I have known you broke up with him before I called you?"

"So, you think the moment I say, 'Zach and I broke up,' I want another guy an hour later? Are you fucking mental?"

Val's eyes got bigger than a cartoon character's. Then just as quickly, they melted into laughter. "Oh my god . . . you never cuss like that." She laughed.

"Grow up, Val." I flung my hands to my face. "I love him—"

"Who, Nigel?"

I dropped my hands and slammed a fist down on the vanity. "Zacharia, you moron. What is going on with you? I just met Nigel."

I spun around and faced the wall, feeling a very ugly cry coming on. "I want him back. This was a mistake. I shouldn't be here."

Val's hand slid over my shoulder. That minimal show of support was all it took to let Niagara Falls loose. "You don't know what we had. Something I could have only dreamt of. Zach would do anything for me." A desperate rage washed over me, fearing my relationship with Zach could really be over.

I spun around, tears running down my face, eyes burning from the leaking mascara. "I wanna go home. I need to see if Zach's called me back."

She grabbed my shoulders and yanked me in a bear hug. "Oh, Tatey. I'm sorry. No, I had no clue how much you love him." She backed away, still holding my shoulders. "I'm sorry. You're right, this was a mistake."

Val dampened a few paper towels before handing them to me. "You might want to clean up before you go out there. I'll go get your purse." I took the moist towels and looked in the mirror. Black mascara ran down my cheeks from my eyes, causing an irritating red. I was a hot mess.

While I dabbed at the black streams, Val came back in. She helped powder my face, and within minutes, you wouldn't have known I'd had a breakdown in the Denny's restroom.

Val stood back, forcing a grin. "We should go out there. You look fine."

I glanced in the mirror and I did look "fine"—it wasn't going to get any better. I tossed the purse over my shoulder, and we went back to the table.

Both guys looked at me and just as fast turned away. Yup, a hot mess.

Val and I took our seats, and I got money out to pay my share of the bill. I went to toss a ten down and Nigel blocked me by waving his hand.

"No, please, Tatum. Let me pay. I appreciate your sticking around."

He placed a fifty-dollar bill over the check. We were at Denny's. The check's total for the four of us was only thirty dollars. Was he giving the waitress a twenty-dollar tip?

Scotty gave Nigel money to cover him and Val and they called it even. Nigel did leave the rest. A tip a typical teenager couldn't afford.

We walked out to the car and Nigel hustled to the front door and opened it for me. "Here, Tate."

I supposed I wasn't allowed in back again. I dropped in and noticed Scotty and Val grinning ear to ear. *Assholes.*

Nigel started the car, and it got uncomfortably quiet.

Val cleared her throat. "Tate, do you mind if Nigel drops us off at a friend's house first? They're waiting on us."

The last thing I wanted was to appear more difficult than I already had. Besides, I was a social disaster with swollen red eyes. "Of course not."

Nigel pulled out of the parking lot. "It's just a few minutes down the road, and then I'll take you home. Promise."

For some reason, we glanced at each other and grinned. Was it because we both were victims of bored people? Who knew, but thank god Nigel seemed like a nice enough guy.

A few minutes later, Nigel parked in front of a brick ranch.

Scotty got out. "Sorry, Tate. See ya later."

Val scooted to the front edge of the seat and patted my shoulder. "Tate, call me tomorrow?"

Mom always said if you don't have anything nice to say, then don't say anything at all, so I nodded in response.

Once Val got out of the car, the emptiness closed in around me. The whole evening was nothing but embarrassing.

She'd had no clue how upset I was about my breakup with Zach, so I couldn't blame her for still asking me to go out with her and Scotty. No sense in holding grudges.

Nigel hadn't said a word to me as he drove us away, but he seemed happy. Did anything bother this guy? I wouldn't have been thrilled driving everyone around while others got to hang out. He was my chauffeur. Awkward.

Nigel drove out of the subdivision and took the back road toward my side of town. This would be a long drive if I didn't say something. Someone had to make the first step.

"Thanks again for taking me home. Like I said earlier, I broke up with a great guy today, and it's not easy for me right now." I still couldn't say those words without feeling heavy-eyed. The slightest thought of Zach broke my heart over and over again.

If Val wouldn't be there for me, maybe this stranger would. "It hurts bad."

Nigel kept his eyes on the road. "I had someone a year ago. That breakup hurt, too. Thought I knew her. Thought we were perfect together. I couldn't have been more wrong."

He didn't glance at me. I watched and waited, but he never looked at me. "Did you tell her you loved her?" I asked.

"Sure." He snuck a quick peek at me. "How 'bout you? Did you tell this bloke you loved him?"

"Oh, yeah. I'm hopeful we can work this out between us."

We both sat there like sappy lost souls. Neither one of us said a word for a minute, which felt like years.

"Nigel?"

"Yeah?"

"Where are you from? I can't ignore your accent." What girl didn't love a British accent?

He chuckled. "Surrey, England. My father is English. My mother is American. They met in an airport, of all places. Dad was a Virgin Airlines pilot. Mom was a stewardess."

"Oh, wow. Love in the air." For the first time in days, I felt lighter. It was nice to just chat. "So they met and fell in love?"

He shot another glance in my direction. "Yeah, something like that."

"Is your dad still flying?"

"No. Dad died years ago. We moved here when I turned twelve to be closer to Mom's side of the family." When he said *Mom*, it came out *Mum*. "Leaving my home in the UK behind."

Of course I would continue to bug him about a difficult subject. Never seemed to fail, open mouth and insert foot.

He glanced over at me. "Mum remarried a few years back. He's a good chap . . . has to be to put up with us." Nigel laughed.

"I'm sorry. How old were you when your dad died?" That slipped, never meant to get so personal. "Sorry, too far."

"Nah. No worries." Nigel shook his head. "I'm fine. Dad died when I was four. My sister knew him. I really didn't get a chance to."

"Well, we know how to keep a conversation light, don't we?"

He looked at me and laughed. "It's probably best to steer clear of my family or background then."

"Oh boy . . . don't I know the feeling."

Even though we both ended on a laugh, you could feel the heartbreak in the car. I felt Nigel might have been as broken as I was.

"So how did your parents meet?" Nigel glanced in the rearview mirror. "You know about mine, tell me about yours."

"Oh . . . you'll be on antidepressants by morning, but if you must know—" We both chuckled. "My dad was actually a small-time boxer, back in the day."

"Really? A boxer?"

"Uh yeah, why is that so funny?"

"You never hear that, it's brilliant. Bet your dad isn't one to screw with." Nigel looked up into the rearview mirror again.

"No. Believe it or not, my mom's the one you don't screw with. Anyway, Mom worked at the diner next door to the gym. I quickly became the "oops," and they married. Dad stopped fighting and took a factory job to support our family. Nothing exciting."

To me, it wasn't a fascinating story, but Nigel seemed to get a kick out of hearing my dad used to punch people for a buck.

"So, your dad knocked up your mum between knockouts?" He busted out into laughter, tossing his hand up. "I'm sorry. That's a lame joke."

Maybe, but I could appreciate it. He had a contagious laugh and I found myself joining him. "Anyhow, since I was their 'oops,' I've always felt like my mom was mad that I was here. It's fine. I had Grandma, who mostly raised me so Mom could work."

Nigel sobered and glanced over at me. "Sorry you're not close with your mother."

"No I'm not. That's okay, it worked out for the best

anyway. Grandma and I were best friends." This chat had taken an ugly turn again.

He took another look in his mirror, but this time he watched. His behavior made me check the passenger's side-view mirror. There was a car behind us, but nothing out of the ordinary. "Nigel, is everything okay?"

He kept taking quick glances out the front window before watching behind us. "You said you broke up with that boyfriend today, right?"

"Yeah, why?"

Nigel looked me right in the eyes. "What kind of car does he drive? A car? Truck?"

Not wasting a second, I twisted in my seat toward the back window. Zach wouldn't be so controlling to do such a thing as follow me. "Zach didn't even know I was leaving the house." I heard Nigel giving the big Mercedes a little more gas. "I can't tell what kind of car it is, the lights are in my eyes." The car wasn't low like Zach's, and not as wide.

"It looks like a Ford Taurus type car, a sedan. Bloody hell, the lights are in my eyes too."

I turned around. "I don't think it's Zach's car. We'd hear it."

"Maybe it's nothing, but they've been on my arse since we dropped Scotty and Val off."

I held my laughter in, he didn't pronounce ass like American do.

Nigel turned down my street. We both watched as the car behind us kept going. We got a look at it from the side when it passed.

"Yup, a Ford Taurus, all right." Nigel grinned, as if he was proud of himself for calling what kind of car it was.

All I cared about was knowing if it was Zach or not. And it wasn't.

"Tatum, I'm sorry Val and Scotty did this to you tonight. I think we could be friends under different circumstances."

"Agreed."

Nigel parked in front of my house. "Here you are."

"Yep." The house was dark inside. I glanced at my Swatch watch, and it was ten thirty. "Well, this is my stop. Thanks for driving me home."

He ran his hand through his hair. Did every guy do that?

His long bangs relaxed back in place. "Please do not feel obligated—"

*Oh no, don't ruin this, Nigel.*

"Could I call you sometime?" His gaze met mine. "Forget Val and Scotty and their ideas. This is strictly about us being friends. Seems we have some exes in common."

I was positive my ex and his ex were not similar. "Sure. Do you have a piece of paper?" I dug in my purse for a scrap.

"Don't need it, just tell me. I won't forget."

"Okay." A nice guy, but he had no intentions of following through if he didn't write the number down. But that would be fine with me. I rattled off, "867-5309."

Nigel had the most irresistible grin. He looked at me sideways. "Tatum, that's Jenny's number. How about your real number?"

For some reason, Nigel seemed easy to read. My grandma had taught me to read facial expressions and body language, and Nigel showed me a lot. He was sincere. And he thought this was funny. We both busted into laughter at the same time. I didn't care for the song much, but the radio sure seemed to love it since it was on their daily, or hourly, playlist. "Okay, sorry. Just had to." Then I recited my real phone number. I hadn't given him a song title phone number to avoid giving him my real number, I'd done it to be funny, and Nigel had caught me.

I collected my things. "Thanks again for driving me home. See ya around, Nigel." I glanced back at him. He had his forearm resting on the steering wheel. For a split second, I envisioned Zach. I blinked and shook the image out of my head. Continuously imagining Zach put that cinder block back on my chest. The visions were downright stupid of me.

I got out and waved goodbye.

Nigel yelled out the window as he drove off, "See ya, Jenny . . . sorry, I mean Tatum." He waved.

Ha. He seemed to have a great sense of humor.

Suddenly, a sedan similar to the one following us pulled up to the curb, one house down and across the street, and killed the engine. It wasn't a neighbor I knew or recognized.

The driver's door opened. A guy got out. It was Kyle.

My worst nightmare was coming at me. Even in the dark, I could see he looked pissed.

Is it considered breathing when you inhale, but never exhale? I felt my chest rise, but it never fell. My feet wouldn't budge. Even if I ran for the door, I wouldn't make it inside before he got me.

He charged. "You slut. Have you even closed your legs since we were together?"

*"Since we were together*?" Enough was enough. I'd be damned if I'd let him intimidate me. "Is that how

you remember it?"

Kyle laughed. "You know you wanted it."

## CHAPTER 12

*Tatum*

A loud engine roared to life down the street, but I couldn't take my eyes off Kyle and his heavy, bull-like breathing. My feet might not have been able to move, but I could swing my purse off my shoulder and clobber him upside his head. Kyle wouldn't hurt me ever again.

"Bitch, if I can't have you, nobody can," Kyle brought his hand up toward my neck.

I was ready to swing but noticed the car barreling down the street. The familiar rumble stopped Kyle and me. We both looked at the car.

The Camaro squealed to a stop in front of my driveway and Zach jumped out.

Kyle spun around and growled at Zach's presence. "When are you going to stop protecting this slut?"

Zach charged Kyle. "When you fucking get it through your thick skull you'll never touch her again."

I found my feet and hopped back as they both swung at the same time.

Zach slightly ducked to the side, though, avoiding Kyle's fist.

Kyle didn't duck. Zach's fist made contact with Kyle's cheek. His head flew back.

Readjusting his grip on Kyle's shirt, Zach gave Kyle another hard punch. Blood dripped from a fresh cut below Kyle's droopy eyes.

I ran over and grabbed Zach's right shoulder and jerked back. In a forced grunt, I said, "Zach, please, stop. Stop."

Before Zach could slam another fist into Kyle's bloodied face, he paused and looked back at me. His expression was unrecognizable. His beautifully strong features contorted into an anger that was foreign to me. I had never seen Zach so uncontrollable. For the first time ever, I was scared of Zach and what he would do to Kyle.

"Zach, you have to stop. Look at him. You've almost knocked him out."

Zach paused, and his chest heaved. He released Kyle's shirt, flinging him backward. Kyle stumbled, trying to regain his balance.

Zach pointed at Kyle. "If you ever think about laying a hand on her again, I will fucking kill you. She won't stop me the next time."

In a drunken stagger, Kyle took off for his car, holding his bloodied cheek. "You Italian piece of shit." He drove off.

Zach turned to me, and I collapsed into his arms.

With the realization Kyle wanted to seriously hurt me, again, I couldn't stop the ugliest cry of my life. "Oh my god . . . he came to my house . . . he could have—"

Zach squeezed me, his head resting over mine. His heavy breathing vibrated a few strands of my hair. "Shhh, I'll never let him touch you, Tatum," he whispered. "He will never lay a hand on you again. I swear on my mother's life."

The man I loved with my entire soul had saved me. I wanted to be in his arms. I wanted him to never leave me. There was so much love between us I could feel it joyously dancing between our bodies.

Zach cupped the sides of my face and lowered his lips to mine. We embraced for a kiss. The kind of kiss you want and need after realizing what you could have lost.

This was exactly where I belonged.

## CHAPTER 13

### Zach

Good thing Tatum stopped me. I would have killed that asshole. I needed Tatum. She kept me under control.

I pushed Tatum back and held her arms, examining her body from head to toe.

"Are you okay? He didn't touch you? 'Cause if he did—"

She was still trying to catch her breath. "No. Because of you. Oh, Zachy . . . when Nigel drove off I thought—"

"Who?" Tatum had stabbed me in the chest and then shipped me to Italy without even knowing what she'd done.

Her face relaxed. "Oh, umm . . . Nigel."

"Who the hell is Nigel? Were you already out with another fucking guy?" *God damn it, I'm losing control.*

Tatum took two steps back. "No, I wasn't. Now, look . . . Zach . . . I tried to call you a hundred times tonight—"

"So because you can't get ahold of me, you go out with another guy?" I shortened the gap between us. I didn't want to believe she'd do that to us, but would she?

Tatum flung her hands to her hips. "No. Let me finish, hothead. I was in bed when Val called and she heard me . . ." Tatum looked down at my feet.

"Say it. She heard you what?"

She looked up at me, her eyes filling with tears. "Sniffling. I had been crying all night because I thought you were never going to speak to me again."

"Why would you think that?" I didn't want to see her cry. I pulled her into my arms.

"You never answered my calls." Her voice was muffled against my shirt.

I released her. "You forget, I'm the one committed to you. I've been busy with family." Crap. The last thing we needed to talk about was my family. She'd go running again. "So, Val called and heard you crying?"

"Yeah. So, I told her why and she blurted out that she and Scotty were picking me up in twenty minutes. But it wasn't just her and Scotty. They'd brought one of his friends, Nigel."

*Son-of-a-bitch. I put myself at risk with my family and she's out with another guy.*

Tate took a step back. "Zach. I swear to you nothing happened. I was so pissed that Val did that to me . . . I asked Nigel to bring me back home. Trust me, I let my feelings be known to Val and Scotty."

"Did this Nigel guy know your feelings too?" I clenched my jaw to remain calm.

"Zacharia Bertano, how dare you be jealous. You have no right since you didn't answer one of my phone calls. I fricking begged you. Cried to you. I sounded like a lunatic tonight. And you get jealous over something I had no control over. How dare you. And as a matter of fact, I told Nigel all about you."

"What did you say, Tatum?"

"Nothing, just it seems we both have exes in common."

"How could you talk about me? You know better."

She backed up and glanced up at me. Once we made eye contact, she stopped moving and stared at me with a glaring eye. "I would never 'talk' about you or your family. You've flipped your damn irrational lid tonight."

"This Nigel brought you home? Alone?" The fact that she was with this other guy was driving me insane. I trusted her. I didn't trust other guys.

"Yes." Her lips tightened.

"Did he know Kyle was following you?"

"He thought a car was following us. Then we turned off, but the car kept going."

No one could take care of her like I would. "But he drove away before you got to your front door. Any decent guy makes sure the girl makes it inside before they drive off."

"I'm not doing this. I hoped we could work it out, but with everything else going on, I'm not dealing with your imagination running rampant and creating jealousy. I'm tired. Tired of waiting all fricking night for your ass to call me."

"I got here as soon as I could." If I had driven myself to the restaurant, it wouldn't have taken me so long to get to her house.

Tatum took in a deep breath and exhaled. "And thank god you did." She placed her hand on my cheek and took a deep breath. "I appreciate it, Zach."

I ignored her touch, letting the anger brew inside of me. Before I saw Tatum get out of the Mercedes, I had no clue who it was, but one thing was sure, they sat there for a while. I wasn't stupid. What were they doing? "Did he ask for your phone number?"

"Why?"

Her expression gave me the answer I feared. "Answer me, Tatum. Did you give this Nigel your phone number?" I wanted to find this guy and make sure he knew to back off.

"He's a friend. I gave you my number because we were friends."

"I already knew your number. You never had to give it to me. Besides, guys never want to be just friends, Tatum. *Never.*" That last bit came out a little louder than I intended.

Her eyebrows pulled together. "You said before I dated you that you were my friend. Just my friend. Always. Are you saying you lied?"

"I've always wanted to be more than friends. Guys talk to guys or no one. They don't talk to girls. Is that the spiel he gave you? 'Let's be friends, give me your phone number?' Because if so, he lied to you. He only wants in your pants."

She raised her hand to slap me. But I caught her wrist.

Her eyes expanded and she snapped her head up, looking like she'd seen a ghost. Her posture cowered downward. I immediately released her hand.

"Shit. I'm sorry, Tate. I shouldn't have touched your wrists."

She began crying. "Good bye, Zacharia."

Tatum ran to her side door and before I could ask her to wait, I could hear the sound of a deadbolt click.

The situation couldn't be more fucked. I shouldn't have grabbed her wrist like that. But why couldn't she see that being out with another guy while I was in Gramps's office, saving us from his crazy ideas of me marrying some damn Italian princess, was wrong? Damn it, there went my chance. I'd had it in the bag tonight. Had it before she decided to go off and make "friends."

Two hours later, Bobby arrived at Tatum's house. Gave me enough time to gather my thoughts and cool off.

I got out of my car and walked over to Bobby's.

He flung his car door open. "You would think since you're getting the security you wanted, you'd look happier."

"Sorry. You're right. Thanks for doing this, Bob."

He got out of his car, carrying his black bag filled with gadgets and wires. "Hey, no prob, but what happened? Besides the whole Gramps thing. I know about that and your three weeks."

We stood in the middle of the street. I kept my voice down. "Tatum. While I was trying to get Gramps to give me more time, she got a call from her old friend and was out with another guy tonight."

"Shit."

"Yeah, and she gave him her number."

Bobby's eyebrows shot upward.

"You know . . . so they could be *'friends.'*"

Bobby looked at me for a long minute and then laughed. "Seriously? Don't tell me Tatum fell for the 'let's be friends' shit?"

I turned toward her house and walked. I had to believe she gave this Nigel her number because of something else. Something she didn't want to mention to me.

Bobby joined me. "Sorry. I didn't mean anything by—"

"I know, don't worry."

He placed his hand on my shoulder and squeezed. "Zach, stop."

I did, without looking at him.

"Sorry, man, but you need to tell me what's going on."

This couldn't be over fast enough. I recapped the whole story, from the moment the S-Class Mercedes pulled up and Tatum stepped away from our argument.

"Man. So, okay, Kyle is definitely after Tatum. And some Brit has her number—we know he's interested."

My hands flexed in and out, feeling the soreness across my knuckles.

Bobby looked down at my hands. "And now Tatum's pissed at you. Again."

"Genius."

Bobby shook his head, snickering. "Damn, man . . . do you think you could just let this ride out for a day? I know it hurts, but giving Tatum the third degree as if you don't trust her will not get her back."

"I do trust her, but we're not going out anymore. Remember? She can do what she wants with whom she wants."

"Whether you're steady or not, if you keep reacting like an asylum escapee with Tatum, it will push her away faster. Faster than Gramps would leave you in Italy."

"Let's just set this up. I'm tired."

Bobby turned, and we walked toward her house. "Now, this here is a motion sensor. Very tiny. Dad said to put it about four inches below ground."

Bobby held up two thin square-like disc pieces with thinner black wires running from disc to disc. On top of the disc plates were little metal pieces lined in rows, sticking upward. "Not a sensor that will alarm if there's a rabbit or squirrel. A *heavy* presence."

"Great. That's all I need."

"Exactly. No one will stand under her window without making their presence known."

"Good. 'Cause the next time Kyle tries anything, he won't be walking away."

## CHAPTER 14

*Tatum*

Sunday, December 3, 1989

Crying myself to sleep didn't help my eyes the next morning. No matter how much concealer I wore, everyone at work commented about my swollen eyes.

Thankfully, after work I had the house to myself and I could lie in bed with cucumbers over the sleep-deprived eyes of a pathetic single girl.

Murphy's Law—the moment I lay down, cucumbers in place, the damn phone rang. I reached over to my nightstand and found the receiver. "Hello."

"Hi, Tate. It's Andi."

Huh, Andi. Now wasn't that interesting? The only other link between Zach and me was my girlfriend Andi, who was also dating Zach's cousin, Matt. I couldn't help but think Zach was behind this, but if he was, did it matter?

"Hey, what's up?"

"Honestly?" Her voice went cold.

"Of course." *Damn. Damn it. Damn it. I don't want*

*to do this with her.*

"I don't want to get involved—"

"Then don't, Andi. Things are bad enough right now as it is."

"Tatum. I'm not going into the family crap, but could you at least try to work this out with Zach? It's really his last chance."

"Ah, so you heard we broke up?" *Last chance?*

"No. I heard you broke up with him because of their family. Just try—"

My other line began clicking. Although I loved my big-button phone, I never knew who was on the other line.

"Sorry, Andi. My other line. I have to get it because my parents aren't home. Hold on, be right back."

I didn't wait for her to answer, I reached over for the button and pressed down. "Hello?"

"Uh, hi, is this Tatum?" A guy's voice with a British accent said.

I flung myself upright, dropping the cucumbers into my lap. "Uh, yes, who's this?" I knew who it was by the accent and voice, but I needed him to say it. Besides, did I want to sound like I remembered him?

"It's Nigel. Are you available?"

*Available? I'm not going anywhere.* "Sorry? For what?"

He chuckled, "Oh, right. Umm . . . can you talk?"

"Oh yeah, sure." *Dang it, Andi's on the other line talking about Zach. But just because she was talking about Zach shouldn't make me feel as if I'm ignoring him.* "Can you hang on for a minute? Don't go anywhere."

"If this isn't a good time I can—"

"It's fine, wait?"

"Sure," Nigel gently said.

I clicked over. The moment I heard Andi, my heart broke in half and fell to my gut. I shouldn't have felt bad—it wasn't Zach. I wasn't giving up on him, I was giving up on Andi. "Hey, Andi. I gotta take this call."

"Call me back?"

"Sure, I'll call ya right back." I clicked the receiver. "Hello, Nigel?"

"Um no, Tate . . . it's still me, Andi. Who's Nigel?" And then I heard her suck in the deepest breath.

Shit. That stupid crappy old phone. I gave it a death look, because that one slipup would probably be the nail in the coffin for me and Zach. I loved Andi, but she wouldn't keep her mouth shut. "No one, I thought you were hanging up?"

"I was, but then I heard you say something. Then I heard you call me Nigel."

"Okay. I gotta go . . . I'll call you back." I hung up this time. Hung up all the way, meaning I put the phone down on the receiver. The phone rang and I grabbed it.

"Hello?"

"Tatum?" Nigel said.

I could breathe again. "Yes, so what's up?" I lay back down. But my breathing was fast and my chest hurt. Was this really going to happen? Zach said guys never wanted to be "just friends." So I had to find out if he was right or not. And my goal was to prove Zach wrong. Besides, he'd stepped over the line saying Nigel was only interested in getting in my pants. Did Zach think that was the only thing guys wanted me for?

"Nothing much. Just wanted to say thanks again for sticking it out for as long as you did last night."

"Oh, sure. It made me realize I have to always question Val's ideas. I'm just not going to entertain *any* of that right now."

"Oh."

In that one word, I could hear the defeat in Nigel's voice. Was Zach right? Damn it. Surely his response didn't mean anything. "So, what do you have going on the rest of the day, Nigel?"

"Just dinner with my family. Nothing special. You?"

Nigel and I talked for almost an hour on the phone. In that time we got to know about each other's friends, my job, family, music, school, and hobbies. We had more in common than I'd imagined.

"Well, this was great, Nigel. Thanks for listening to me rattle on."

"Sure, whenever."

We both fell silent for the first time in an hour. I knew it was time to end this, but how? He was a nice guy, but I didn't owe him anything. It wasn't about owing anyone, though. It was about being friends. Right?

"Tatum, may I call you next weekend?"

"Of course, whenever." Talking on the phone was harmless.

"If you don't have any plans for the weekend maybe we could do something. The mall on Saturday?"

That's right, he knew I liked the mall, but going out together . . . not so harmless. "Let's see, okay?"

"Of course. Take care."

"You too. See ya, Nigel."

I couldn't help but laugh as I put the phone down. The sad fact was, with his accent I could have let him talk forever. And the last thing I wanted to feel when I got off the phone with him was happy. Light. Carefree.

I felt Nigel was a normal guy, with a normal family. Zach? Zach was nothing normal, but I loved that about him. My heart began beating faster. I wished Zach and I could have had a great conversation for an hour. But whenever we talked the conversation always went to his family.

I would have loved it if he had just called me. But he never did. What was the one damn thing I told him had upset me last night—he never called? Guess Zach didn't listen to a word I said about how I'd waited for him. But if you asked my mom if guys really listened to us, she'd laugh in your face. Not sure why I'd believed Zach would be different.

On the bus ride to school the next morning I applied more makeup around my swollen eyes. Christy said how horrible I looked. She looked radiant as always, but she hadn't cried herself to sleep like I had.

I headed for the main hall where my locker was and slowed down once I made it to our section. Looking desperate to anybody, but especially to Zach, was sad to me. I could be desperate, I just couldn't show it—and I was insanely desperate to see him.

My locker was coming up. There were too many students around. This was not the way to start a new week—scared to death.

The wall where Zach typically stood was bare. But it was unsettling how I could feel someone watching me. I glanced around and didn't see who it could have been. I got to my locker and not only was Zach not there, neither was Andi.

But Diane was.

Disappointment was a nasty pill to swallow. "Hey, Di. What's happening?" I twisted and turned the locker combination.

She leaned her shoulder against the wall and faced me. "I know about you and Zach."

It hurt snapping my head so fast in her direction. "How do you know?"

Diane leaned into me. "My dad talked to Nicola over the weekend and he mentioned his son's ragazza problems was the next—"

"Ragazza? What the hell is that?" I couldn't roll my tongue like Diane could. It was no secret I sucked at any foreign language. Hell, I could barely speak English.

Diane shook her head and chuckled. "Girl. Girl problems. Evidently Nicola is pretty worried about Zach."

Did everyone have to know my business? I hit my forehead on the locker. "This. Isn't. Happening."

Diane put her hand on my shoulder. "It is. But when my dad talked to me last night, we thought there was something else going on with Nicola that he didn't mention."

I stopped and looked at her. "What do you mean?"

"Like, he's not just worried about the breakup." She paused and glanced around before continuing. "It's more than a broken heart. It's a serious devastation to Nicola and Zach. Why? We don't know." She shook her head. "Something more serious is going on with that family, Tate. Real serious."

"Maybe it's about his Uncle Sergio?"

"Nah, they worked that out already. They had to."

I collected my things and shut the locker. "Okay, then I have a feeling Andi is off with Matt and she knows something I did. Not that it's a big deal, but she's told Zach. I'm sure of it."

Diane's eyebrows scrunched, making her dad's old plastic black glasses slide down her nose.

She adjusted the empty frames. "Oh god, tell me, quick."

"Why?"

"Because it could be what they're worried about."

"Oh, right." I filled her in as fast as I could about Kyle. Nigel. And Zach beating Kyle's face in, again. Then I quickly threw in how I hung up with Andi to talk to Nigel.

Diane let out a big exhale. "I'm not sure if that's it. I mean, it's bad, but not like life and death. We got the impression it was life-changing. Anyhow . . ."

We began walking to class.

"Now, tell me about this Brit, Nigel. He sounds yummy!"

## CHAPTER 15

**Zach**

*Monday, December 4, 1989*

Before I stepped off the plane at the Guglielmo Marconi airport in Italy, I glanced at my watch. It was noon in St. Louis, so Tatum was just going to lunch. Bob was supposed to tell her where Gramps had shipped me to. Shipped me to Italy without any fucking warning.

When Gramps gave the orders to put me on the next flight, I had an hour to pack my bags and get to the airport. Dad didn't leave my side, giving me his and Mom's plan the whole time. One of the many things he said was, *Show them you are their equal, not their servant.*

The sun setting in Italy was bright. My eyes adjusted to the light glaring off the glass at the gate, and I noticed Uncle Vito and Aunt Rosalie there waiting for me. Uncle Vito, who looked a lot like my father, didn't appear happy to see me. Aunt Rosalie, on the other hand, couldn't smile enough and had tossed her arms up, waiting for me to hug her.

"Zacharia. Welcome, my dear!" Aunt Rosalie said in a grunt from squeezing me so hard.

Rosalie was so short I had to duck to hug her. "Hi, Aunt Rosalie." I backed away and stepped over to Vito. I stood as tall as I could. Looking sad and pathetic to Vito wouldn't help me. Not only was I representing myself, I was representing my father.

He took his free hand and patted my shoulder. "Zacharia, let's get you to the manor and get you settled. We talk about this girl spoken for."

This was Gramps's big plan to get me to rescind Tatum. They had no clue what they were in for if they expected me to do that. I'd never break. Dad and I had a plan.

For the next half hour, I rode in my uncle's Mercedes into the countryside, passing vineyard after vineyard. No matter how much I hated being away from Tatum, the land in Italy was beautiful. Tatum would like it. She wasn't much of a city girl.

Uncle Vito drove down the narrow, tree-lined road for miles until we arrived at the black wrought-iron Mediterranean gates. Their watchman welcomed them back and let them enter. The gates were wide enough for a semi to get through, and they connected to a twelve-foot-tall fence that wrapped around the property.

Uncle Vito drove down the cobblestone drive that wrapped behind the house to a four-car garage. It was custom to stay in the car until the garage door shut. Vito was overly cautious, and I didn't want to know why.

Aunt Rosalie wanted me to take my usual room since the rest of the family was scheduled to arrive in two in a half weeks for the holidays.

I stepped in "my" room upstairs and gently shut the door behind me. Letting my bag slide off my shoulder, I chucked it at the bed.

I didn't want to be in Italy. Everyone in the family seemed to understand that but Gramps. Why couldn't he see I needed to be home, St. Louis home, to get me and Tate back together? Because he didn't want me with her. He wanted me to marry Mariacella. But I would never be with anyone other than Tate.

I flopped down on the bed and stared at the arched ceiling. If Gramps putting me on the red-eye wasn't punishment enough, he'd stripped me of my mobile and any communications from Tatum. He'd even told Vito to supervise my phone calls to my parents. If he hadn't done this to me, I could have tried to salvage what Tatum and I had. I was a fucking prisoner.

The intercom on the nightstand clicked on. "Zacharia, dear, Vito *ti vuole nel suo ufficio* (wants you in his office)."

I wanted to yell out *Fuuuuuuck.*

Instead I said I'd be right there.

I held my head high and walked down the Italian marble hall. It had a nice muted echo of my footsteps. I knocked on Vito's office door, and he called to enter. Vito's office wasn't anything like Gramps's. Cream walls and almost black woodwork with black iron fixtures decorated the room. It wasn't as intimidating as Gramps's office, that was for sure.

Vito did throw his hand toward his chairs like Gramps. "Zacharia, son, *siediti.*"

The moment my ass hit the seat, I knew this would be my hardest fight ever.

## CHAPTER 16

*Tatum*

Come lunchtime, Zach still wasn't in school, and neither was Andi. Maybe they were both at home sick.

I went by Zach's cousins' lockers, the ones that circled the cafeteria dining floor. When I turned the corner, a hand grabbed my shoulder and tugged back.

Kyle was after me. I jerked my head away, causing me to stumble back from the force.

"Tate, wait." Thank god it was only Bobby. Relief showered me.

Looking up at him, I straightened my clothes. "What are you doing? You scared the piss out of me."

"We need to talk. Follow me."

He escorted me outside in front of the school and sat on a bench. I sat next to him. He didn't even take a peek in my direction. No eye contact was a bad sign. But I didn't take my eyes off of him even though it was cold and I wanted to tell him to hurry up.

He stared out into the parking lot. "This won't be easy, so hear me—"

"Just spill it, Bob." He was wasting my time. I had

to see if Zach was sick or not.

"Fine." He finally looked at me. His big eyes pierced mine. "Zach's in Italy. Plain and simple—"

I froze. In Italy? That was crazy. Zach had to be home, sick.

"Don't look at me like I'm lying. I'm not."

Probably all an elaborate game to get me to back off. Nope. I wouldn't believe it for one second. Zach wouldn't up and leave me.

"He left yesterday, Tatum. After Gramps heard about this Nigel and Kyle." Bobby's eyebrows scrunched together. "Zach won't be back until he rescinds his commitment to you. And fair warning, he told us all he'd die before he rescinds."

Confusion made my mouth drop open. I didn't want to believe it, but why would Bobby lie? Not sure he was, but still, that was easier than admitting the truth.

"It's going to be a long time before he returns, Tate. If ever. Do you hear me?"

Time froze. The school grounds were quiet. Even the dead leaves on the trees were still. No cars coming or going. No birds chirping. Silence. I was alone in a soundproof bubble. Zach had left me. I felt like someone had taken a sledgehammer to my gut.

Bobby's words kept playing over in my head. *Gramps heard about this Nigel and Kyle. Zach won't be back until he rescinds his commitment to you.*

*Zach's gone? Really gone?* I glanced up at Bobby. "You're serious?"

He nodded.

No, this could not be happening! I turned to look out into the parking lot, and the silence of my surroundings confirmed I was alone. Was he forced to leave me? Or did he just want to be far away from me?

I stood and began walking to the front door, feeling like a heartless zombie on a bad day.

"Tate? Wait, please," Bobby called out as he ran in front of me, looking as bad as I felt. "There's nothing I can say to make you feel better—"

My nostrils flared. "Feel better?" Was he insane? Nothing would make me feel better but having Zach back, and that didn't sound like a possibility.

Bobby took a step back from me. "I'm on your side. Your's and Zach's side. Even Zach's parents don't agree with Gramps's tactics on this."

"So this is all Gramps's doing? Zach had nothing to do with it?"

Bobby's shoulders slumped. "Yeah. Tatum, Gramps originally gave Zach until the twenty-second. We leave for our holiday visit to Italy in less than three weeks. And if you didn't speak for Zach by then, Gramps was leaving him in Italy anyway."

There was no way I wanted to breathe anymore. My life, my everything was gone. "So basically, I had three lousy weeks before Zach was being made to move to Italy?"

"Yes. That's why Zach showed up late Saturday night. He was trying to get more time from Gramps, knowing the family leaves soon anyway."

*You forget, I'm the one committed to you. I've been busy with family. I got here as soon as I could.* That had to be what Zach had been talking about. I remembered our last kiss. Our last embrace. Zach had me convinced that he wanted me and everything would be okay. Those visions washed away.

No escaping our coffin now—it was nailed shut. A tightness closed around my chest like a vice.

Zach was gone. Gone? I couldn't look at Bobby's

face one more second. I took off inside the school and ran. Just ran. Toward anywhere there wasn't a person around.

*This can't be happening. Damn it. Gramps controls everything and everyone, like I feared from the beginning. I was right. I didn't speak for Zach, and the old man still ruined my life. And Zach's.*

I couldn't get home fast enough after school. In my driveway, I could hear the phone ringing. I fumbled for my key and threw the door open as fast as I could. If only it was Zach.

I flipped the receiver up. "Yes, hello?"

"I got your note," Diane was more out of breath than me. "Oh dear god, Tatum. They shipped him to Italy? This is it, this is the ragazza problems."

"Yeah, and it's all because I took that fucking phone call from Nigel. And stupid fucking Kyle."

"Oh Tate, don't. If that's all it took . . . Zach was going to be left behind anyway, unless you spoke for him. Would you have done that in three weeks?"

"Well, not sure that's the point. Hold on, I'm switching phones." I ran into my bedroom and tossed my backpack on the waterbed and picked up the receiver on my nightstand. Then I ran to hang up the living room phone. Back in my room, I sat down on the edge of my bed. "No matter what, this is all my fault. He's there right now because of me."

"I know." Diane took a breath. "I'm sorry. This is just screwed up." She was quiet for a second. Then said, "Tate, this is what you would have been dealing with. God knows this is the last thing you want to hear, but this is why I told you not to rush things with Zach. His Gramps rules everything."

"What do you mean?"

"Look, I know you love Zach, but no matter how much you love him, you are too damn young for living on call. And Gramps would own you. Women work in that family too."

"What do you mean, 'work'?" I slid off the waterbed frame down into the rippling mattress.

"Once you speak for Zach, you're also working for Gramps. I take it he didn't mention that part?"

"Um, no . . . no . . . he didn't." Zach didn't mention anything about what it really meant to speak for him. What kind of work? Work at their restaurant? Or dirty work?

"I'm sorry, Tate."

"Yeah, me too." My head felt heavy. My chest. My body. Sinking. "Diane, I gotta go. Sorry. I'm just not feeling well."

"Of course. Call me if you need anything. I'm here."

"You're the best, Di. Thanks."

The house was silent but for Gizmo's claws scraping on the floor as he padded into my room and stared at me. "He's gone, Gizzy." Gizmo's rear end flopped down. "Zachy's gone."

The words were a hand across my face. I collapsed on my bed and let all of my regret out. Gizmo jumped up next to me and rested his chin on my side. We stayed like that until I had no more tears to cry.

## CHAPTER 17

*Tatum*

The next morning Andi was at our locker, her forehead resting against the metal door. Once she noticed my arrival, she stood up and immediately came to life.

"Tatum, I'm so sorry. I had no clue that telling the Bertanos about Nigel's phone call would lead to this."

I put my hand on her shoulder. "I know. How would you have known? And if you did know, that means you really hate me, and we both know that's not the case."

"Oh my god, no. Of course not." Andi's gaze dropped to the floor. "Gramps sent him to Italy." She looked back up at me with puppy dog eyes that clawed at my heart, and they shouldn't have. "It's all screwed up. Nicola and Catalina are beside themselves. I feel bad. If I would have kept my mouth shut—"

"Andi, have you spoken for Matt?"

Her eyes expanded. "No, not yet. Why?"

I got my stuff out of the locker. "You need to make damn sure this is what you want."

"I know." Andi thudded her back against her locker. "Trust me, I fear Gramps will be on us next. He clearly has issues with them dating people and not getting the commitment in return."

"That's not the problem." I slammed my locker shut. "This is way more than committing. Because I was committed to Zach. This is about agreeing to be in Gramps's family, forever. And I'll be damned if I join the Mob."

For the next week, life as I knew it was over. It wasn't easy—actually, it was one of the most painful things I'd been through, but I got through the week without Zach. This ranked up there with losing my grandma. Now I'd lost Zach too.

Andi and Diane did what they could to support me, but all I cared to do was work.

*Saturday, December 9, 1989*

This was not the weekend to have Saturday evening off. I was so pathetic I even called Saturday's crew beforehand and asked if anyone wanted off, but they all wanted the money for the holidays. It wasn't about the money for me.

My family left for a Chuck E. Cheese's night out with Toni. Any other time I would have loved to be alone, but not now.

I stood at the front door and stared out, fantasizing about Zach driving down the street. Just thinking about him made him seem closer.

But another car caught my attention. It was a newer Mazda with dark tinted windows. So dark you couldn't see in. I was sure having them that tinted was illegal in Missouri.

Concentrating so hard on the Mazda, I jumped four inches in the air when the phone rang.

Forgetting all about the car, I ran for the phone. Praying again it was Zach. "Hello?"

"Uh, Tatum, it's Nigel."

A million things went through my mind. The most important was, he was the last shoulder I needed to cry on. Nigel had this calming effect on me, and I didn't trust myself not to open up to him. "Hi, Nigel. How are you?"

"Oh, fine. Umm, just curious if you were available tonight?"

Again with his English accent. It was cute, though. "Maybe. What do you have in mind?"

"Nothing special, the mall?"

It came down to two options. Obviously, one was to go out with him. The second was to sit home and cry to Gizmo the rest of the night. "Sure. Can you pick me up?"

"Is half an hour okay?"

"Yeah, see ya then."

I freshened my makeup and checked my wallet for cash. A knock came at the front door within half an hour. Right on time. I wrote a note to my parents about where I would be, and then grabbed my purse and coat. Gizmo whined at me, so I paused mid-step.

"Oh, don't . . . what am I supposed to do? Zach's in Italy, for Christ's sake. Just don't." I stepped around the dog. "I can't sit here and wait forever. I was warned he isn't coming back any time soon, if ever. He's gone, Gizzy." My throat burned at saying those words. The damn dog was going to make me cry.

Before getting to the door, I made sure to swallow the lump.

Nigel stood there with his hands in his jean pockets. "Hi, Tatum."

I wanted to laugh at how nervous he seemed. "Hi. I'm ready."

Nigel jogged ahead and opened the car door for me. We were alone. I wasn't sure if Val and Scotty were in on this or not, but it appeared as if Nigel was acting of his own free will this time.

It was relatively quiet between us walking through the mall. Nothing caught my attention in the windows. Good for my wallet. Festive Christmas decorations hung everywhere, but my mood could be described as anything *but* festive. A heavy sigh escaped my lips.

"Tatum, are you okay?" Nigel peered around to see what was wrong.

"Yeah. I'm sorry, it's just been a shitty week for me."

"Do you wanna talk about it?"

I looked into another passing storefront. "Nah. It's kind of private." I tried not to meet his eyes for fear that I might start crying. "But thanks for asking."

"Did you eat dinner?"

"Nah, but I'm fine."

Nigel grabbed my hand and gently pulled. "Come on, you need to eat."

"Okay. But not Mexican."

His warm touch made me want to pull away because feeling anything nice wasn't allowed. It ruined my bad mood. Not to mention, holding a guy's hand reminded me of Zach. It had been a week since Zach had touched me, but it felt like years.

He looked back at me, escorting me into a mall restaurant. "My treat." His face lit up with satisfaction.

Nigel wasn't allowing me to pout anymore. He sat

across from me at the small table.

As we sipped on our cherry Cokes, he said, "This may sound corny, but I like the holidays. How 'bout you?"

His adorable smile got me every time. "Sure, I like them. So do you travel for the holidays then?"

He cocked his head to the side, but I suppose that was a weird question to ask him. I had to see if there were any similarities between him and Zach, though.

"No." Nigel chuckled. "Do you?"

"Ha. My parents are too cheap to do anything like that. But considering it's our first Christmas without my grandma, it won't be very jolly." Especially since Zach wouldn't be there either. I hated the holidays.

"Without your grandma?"

"Sorry. My grandma died earlier this year. The one I mentioned who kind of raised me so mom could work."

"Right. I'm sorry. I understand how it feels to lose someone you love. It may sting less as time goes on, but the pain never goes away."

Damn it I didn't want to cry in front of him. No matter how hard I tried to avoid Nigel's gaze, our eyes did meet. I saw his soft and caring grin. He really understood how I felt.

Nigel reached over the table and held my hand. "Why don't you spend Christmas Eve with me? I'd love to have you over. Just as friends if you prefer."

Cherry Coke got caught in my throat, and I gave my chest a few solid pats to get the lump down. "Go to your house? For Christmas?"

"Yeah, why not? We do a family gathering on Christmas Eve, and then for New Year's Eve, my sister and I throw a party at my parents other house. You can be my guest for both."

"Other house?" I couldn't think fast enough. He was throwing one question at me after another.

"Yeah, we have two. One we live in and one we just store extra stuff in. Extra furniture, really. The belongings of my father's that my mom can't throw out are stored there. It's his house, really."

That would suck to constantly be reminded of your loss. "Maybe, let's see." This was too much, too soon. "Do you honestly like me?" Not sure what made me do it, maybe it was the fact my heart was deflating with each passing day, or that I hadn't heard from Zach. I didn't want to be hurt again.

He cocked his head to the side, examining me. Then he twisted his mouth. He relaxed back into his chair. "Of course I do. But what's really going on?"

"What do you mean, 'what's really going on'? I'm just curious."

Nigel shook his head and leaned forward and stared me in the eye, looking right through me. He didn't blink. "This guy really screwed with your head, didn't he?"

"Who?" Was he referring to Kyle? But he didn't know Kyle.

"Uh, your ex. I think you mentioned his name was Zach."

"Sorry." I took a deep breath and sat back in my chair. "Zach is off-limits right now."

Nigel took a bite of his food, relaxing. "Say no more. Life sucks, that's for damn sure. But I'm here whenever you need me."

I knew he meant what he said. The tension dissipated between us.

The rest of dinner flew by because Nigel was so easy to talk to. He was one of those guys you could talk to about any subject and he'd know a little or a lot about it. Then there was music. We had the love of music in common, but we were both picky. He was surprised I liked The Cure. But even better, we both disliked Tiffany Gibson. We sipped on cherry Cokes, talking about the Pixies' new album. It was reassuring to be so relaxed and carefree with him. I wasn't worried about him flying off the handle if I glanced up and there just so happened to be a guy walking by, like I had been with Kyle. Nor was I concerned about what the Mob was doing and if they were indirectly affecting my life, like I was with Zach. Everything was normal.

After we ate, Nigel drove me home. He parked in front of the house. "No matter what happened, you did great going out tonight."

"Thanks, but we both know I'm lame."

"Nah, you're just going through something. I get it." He put his hand on my shoulder. "I swear I do."

The energy coming off his hand was all it took to get me to open my big mouth. Exactly what I'd feared. Maybe it was a subconscious feeling that I could trust him and that he understood more than I was giving him credit for.

"Zach left me. Like left me forever."

In the dark I could still see his eyes narrow inward. "Are you sure? Maybe he just wants a break?"

I looked away, feeling the damn tears coming. "No mistake, he's on permanent vacation. I was warned by others he's even left town."

"Jesus. Really? He moved? You can't still keep in touch?"

I laughed, tears running down my face. "I wish it were that simple. Trust me." The ugly cry came barreling out. The more I spoke of Zach leaving me, the more it became real. And reality sucked.

"Hey. Hey, it's okay." Nigel shuffled around in the glove box and handed me a tissue. "Here."

I wiped my eyes. "Thanks."

Nigel put his arms around me, letting me rest my forehead on his chest. "Just so you know, I didn't tell Val or Scott about asking you out tonight. I don't want them involved anymore."

"Thank you. I appreciate that." I was glad to have that confirmed. The comfort was back. I searched his face. "Thanks for dinner."

"No prob."

His James Dean eyes were soft and gentle and showed he cared more than I wanted him to at the moment. It was time to leave before he heard more about me and Zach.

I got out of the car and waved goodbye.

This time, he didn't take off so quickly. He didn't know about Kyle, but I did. And I watched the neighborhood around me. Down the street, in a different location, sat the same Mazda from earlier. It was too dark to see more than I had before. I hustled up to the door since Nigel appeared to be waiting on me. At the door, I turned and waved goodbye and stepped inside. I could hear the big Mercedes drive off.

I tiptoed to my room and looked out the window and down the street. The Mazda was rolling toward my house, lights off. I jerked away from my window shades, gasping. Damn. I feared Kyle was following me again. But that wasn't his car. The windows . . . they were dark. Like Zach's. I peeked through the mini-blinds again. The car had stopped one house down. *What's going on?* Not taking any chances, I made sure the windows were locked.

Gizzy strolled into my bedroom. "Gizmo, get up here." He hopped up in bed with me.

My heart was beating fast. I didn't mean to panic, but Zach was gone. There was no one to help me if Kyle did try something. I was alone.

Then I remembered Zach's words, *Keep these windows locked, and Gizmo up in bed with you.* Did he know this would happen? How could he have known?

## CHAPTER 18

### Zach

*Wednesday, December 13, 1989*

The Bertano Manor's garage was a tight fit for Uncle Vito's new Mercedes. Just the two of us were in the car, so this was a good time to speak up.

"Uncle Vito, I have a favor to ask. Just hear me out first—"

"Zach, Gramps gave me strict rules not to let you use the phone to call Tatum."

Vito was eyeing both sides of his doors, his fault for buying the biggest Mercedes built.

This dance with them was exhausting. "I know, but I've proven I'm committed here. I've turned in my studies back home. I've done everything you guys have wanted me to. Can't I call her? In the States, even the criminals get at least one phone call to whoever they want."

Vito laughed as he pressed on the parking brake and turned off the ignition. "I'm not too old to understand the pain you experience, Zacharia. But do you know what Gramps will do if he finds out?"

"How would he find out?"

Uncle Vito looked around with an I'm-stuck-in-the-middle grin. "If Gramps sees your spoken for's number on the bill, he'll kill me. Find another way."

"How?"

He closed the garage door and got out of the car. "You're smart, find another way."

I jumped out of the car, not allowing him to walk away from me before he agreed to a damn phone call. "Then can I use your phone in the office and you monitor my call to Bobby? I want to talk to him to see how things are going."

Vito walked toward the door, not giving me the time of day. "I will supervise."

Hours later, we went into Vito's office and he dialed Sergio's house. Bob answered, but Matt was with him, so he got on the other phone. It was my lucky day.

"Listen, they still won't let me call her. So I have to be creative." I glared over at Uncle Vito standing in the doorway. He didn't look back at me. The bastard just smiled.

"So now we're going to be your messengers?" Bob snickered.

"Don't. It's hard enough for him and Tate as it is," Matt said.

"Oh, I'm just joking. Of course, Zach. Whatever you want."

"First, how is she? What has she been up to?" I had to hurry, no telling if Vito would cut my call short. He stood there, still grinning.

"Shitty." Bob wasn't laughing. "I've never seen her look so bad. Her eyes are constantly red and swollen—"

Huh? She looked bad? What was happening to her?

"Bob, stop," Matt cut in. "She's okay, as good as you'd expect. I've talked to Andi and she's going to be with Tate more."

"Well, did Andi do something with her this weekend?" Tatum needed her girlfriends.

The line was silent.

"Bob? Matt? Did I lose you?"

"No, we're here," Bob said.

"Okay. Can someone answer me? What did she do this weekend? Work?" I felt my nerves burn. They were testing my patience. Or were they too damn afraid of their answers. Shit.

"Zach, she did work, but she went out Saturday evening for a few hours too," Matt said.

That sounded more like it. "Good, she needs to stay busy. So did she go out with Andi or Val?" So far, Tate was holding up. I knew she would, she was tough.

Again, nothing.

"Damn it, hurry up. I don't have all day," I growled. What was their fucking problem? How hard was it to answer direct questions? My clock was ticking.

Uncle Vito turned back and looked at me. His face showed no expression. It meant he didn't like what he was hearing.

"She went out with Nigel Saturday night," Bob answered.

"Nigel? She's out with fucking Nigel again?" I didn't mean to yell that at them.

My heart sank.

Vito didn't look at me. He raised his wrist and looked at his watch, then walked off.

I was dead. Just like that, my big mouth was keeping my ass in Italy.

"Zach, don't worry. I said Andi will get more

involved. She'll spend more time at Tate's house, I promise."

"Yeah, and I'll still monitor the Kyle situation. Everything is fine here," Bobby said.

I barely had the energy to talk. "Did you tell her I wasn't coming back until I've rescinded with the family?"

"Yeah, she took it okay. Did you want us to tell her anything else? Are you okay? You sound tired all of a sudden."

"Vito heard," I whispered. "I just fucked up."

In unison Matt and Bobby said, "Ooh."

"No, just let it go for now."

Bobby took a deep breath into the phone. "Zach, with you stuck there and her moving on . . . I know you love her, but how is that going to work for you?"

"I'll deal with it. I'm coming home after the holidays—"

"How are you going to—"

"I have my ways, Bobby." I had to keep my voice down to barely a whisper. "Trust me . . . I'll be back in St. Louis January second, 1990. Matt, you just get Andi to do her share while I'm gone and Bob, you stay on Kyle. When I get home, I'm fixing me and Tate. Whether this fucking Nigel is in the picture or not."

## CHAPTER 19

*Tatum*

*Friday, December 22, 1989*

Two more weeks passed and here it was the last day before our winter break, and it couldn't be over soon enough. This was my third week without any contact from Zach. And it was still as painful as the day I found out he was gone. Time doesn't heal. Time only drove me crazier. I felt like Ozzy Osbourne, a raging lunatic. One minute I was fine because of school distractions, then the next, I wanted to kill something—my poor foot against the wall sufficed.

As if crappy weeks couldn't bother anyone else, Christy, my Farrah Fawcett neighbor, informed me she was moving. Her father was being relocated, and they were moving during the holiday break from school.

There was one thing I looked forward to that kept me sane—spending more time with Nigel. He was in my life, and I was lucky to have him. Because if Zach was too busy for me, at least Nigel made the time. Nigel called me every day after school. Zach hadn't called once since he'd left for Italy. So if he didn't have the time for me, why should I waste my time thinking about him? Then on the other hand, if someone handed me a one-way ticket to Bologna, Italy, I'd take it and go straight to the airport.

I was glad it was our last school lunch until after the New Year. Sitting there for three whole weeks with just Andi and Matt had been a drag. We never talked to each other. If Andi did talk, she would whisper to Matt. She didn't need to worry about making me feel bad. It just was a bad situation. And I never wanted to put her in the middle.

"Tate?" Andi said.

I stopped picking at my salad and looked at her.

"Are you working tonight?"

"No, I'm off tonight. I work tomorrow."

"Let's do something then?"

"Sure." The lettuce tasted disgusting. I pushed the salad off to the side. "Matt, how is he? You know something. And I know you're all leaving for Italy tomorrow." With Zach's family within reach, I did feel closer to him, but they never spoke of him. His cousins behaved as if he didn't exist, and that drove me crazy. I talked about my grandma and she was gone. I didn't understand why they wouldn't talk about Zach.

Andi stared at him. Matt moved around in his seat, looking uncomfortable. "He's okay, Tate."

I slammed my fist down. "What is your problem? All I ask is how he is and you can't say anything more than he's alive? Seriously." They both appeared stunned. I was sick of how people treated me. "I can't take this anymore. You know how he's doing. Why are you acting like it's some big secret?"

Bobby came flying into the chair next to me and sat.

"Hey there, what's going on?"

"Simple. I'm asking Matt how Zach is, and he won't tell me. Can you?"

A light switch flipped. Bobby's eyes showed no emotion as he glared at me. "He's fine. There's really nothing to report."

My patience incinerated, totally went up in smoke. I lowered my voice to a demented growl. "I am losing my cool with you guys. Something's happened. I know it, and you won't tell me. Now, either Gramps is telling you not to, or Zach is doing something you don't want me to know."

"You wanna know so badly?" Bob raised his voice at me.

"Yes, I'm asking."

"In Italy he's being prepped to marry someone else. Gramps wants him to be with an Italian girl. Not you, Tatum."

Bobby's words ripped through my chest, grabbed my heart, and pulled it out. He had to be lying again.

"You heard me." Bobby's voice was cold.

"Zach doesn't love me?" *What is going on?* I began to question my sanity. Zach wouldn't just up and marry someone else. I'd never heard him talk about another girl.

Bobby continued, "In the family, we don't always get what we want."

I could feel my chest rise. My breathing was heavy. I wouldn't let them see me cry. And if I looked at Andi's face, the tears would come pouring out.

"So what are you saying? Zach's honestly marrying someone else? And he's never coming back? What the hell is going on? I'm confused."

"Yes. Why can't you understand that?" Bob's eyes

became iceberg cold.

"Bob, enough," Matt said.

I twisted my napkin and started to shred it in my fingers. "I guess . . . I thought Zach loved me. He always told me no matter what, he'd love me forever."

Bob slammed his fist down on the table.

I jumped and bit my tongue at the same time from fright.

"Move on, Tatum. Just move on. You're not for Zach. He isn't coming back, ever."

A tear escaped. I could feel it. Bobby was being so mean. He'd never treated me like that before. I had to get out of there with the ugly cry coming. Zach had chucked my heart into the Mississippi like some stupid rock. "Okay, I'll move on. Fine. Gramps will never control me. Never." I kept blinking my eyes and grabbed my belongings. I'd never been so embarrassed in my entire life. Another guy had made a fool out of me. "Merry fucking Christmas, assholes."

I couldn't run away fast enough. A few feet away from the table, I overheard Matt say, "Did you have to go that far?"

When the last bell rang, I wasn't the only one celebrating. Obviously we had different reasons. My reason was, I didn't have to see any of the Bertanos until next year. It felt good to think of it as another year before I had to see those jerks again. If Andi and I weren't so close, I would never have to see them again.

I got home and was putting my backpack away when the phone rang. Probably my daily call from Nigel. Pathetic of me, but it felt good to have someone interested in me.

I found myself smiling, again. "Nigel. Hi."

"How are you? Feeling better?"

"I am. Thanks. I appreciate your taking me out the other night. I was in some kind of bad funk." Maybe I was feeling much better after my blow-up at school. Getting some of the frustration out worked wonders. Or maybe it was the simple announcement to the Bertanos that I would never let Gramps control me. At least they knew where I stood.

"I've been there. But I'm curious if you thought about coming over to my place for Christmas Eve?"

"I didn't, because I didn't think you were serious." The line fell silent. "Hello, Nigel?"

"I never bullshit you, Tatum." His accent was strong with those words. "I'll never lie."

"Oh, okay then. Let me ask my parents. Can I get back with you?"

"Of course." His tone sounded relaxed. "Since you're off tonight, how about I take you out?"

Nigel was just the medicine I needed. "I would, but my girlfriend Andi is sleeping over. Another time, soon?" I wanted to spend as much time with him as possible. What had happened at lunch made me realize I needed to surround myself with people who made me feel good. And Nigel made me feel better than good.

"Absolutely, Tatum. How about you call me when you have some free time?"

I laughed. "Yeah, I guess you've been the one calling me."

"I don't want to pester you—"

"Nigel, stop. You're not pestering me. I appreciate your being here. Actually . . . I don't know how I would have survived these past few weeks without you."

"Blimey. Give yourself more credit, Tatum. You would have been fine. You're stronger than you think. But anything I can do. Anything." With the last word, his tone of voice fell. I could imagine his eyes drooping, and his lips tucked. A calm face he'd made many times in the past three weeks when we were together.

Then it hit me. I wanted to see that face. I wanted to see Nigel.

A short while later, my parents had gotten home from work. There wasn't much time to talk to them about Christmas before Andi got there.

The second they took a seat in the living room, I made my entrance. "I have a question for you. So, Val's friend . . ." I thought it would sound better if I put that angle on it. "Scotty's friend Nigel. He asked me if I could go over to his place on Christmas Eve. Is that okay?"

Mom and Dad both looked at me as if they saw ten Tatum's standing in front of them.

Mom scanned my face like she does when she thinks I'm up to no good. "What about Zach? I know you said he's in Italy for the holidays, but you can't tell me he would be okay with you going over to another guy's house for Christmas. What's going on?"

There was no escaping the news forever. But telling my mom and dad they were right about Zach's family and how he might not have options was not on my tell-all list. I'd be damned if I told them just how right they were. "I don't want to go into it, but Zach and I broke up before he left for Italy. I don't want to talk about it."

Dad raised his eyebrows at my mom, but spoke to me. "We're sorry to hear that, Tatum. We don't have plans Christmas Eve, just Christmas Day. So you can go if you want."

If I didn't look away I'd cry, because no matter how stern my mom was, I could see the pity in her eyes.

"Thank you." I ran to my room and locked the door.

## CHAPTER 20

*Tatum*

*Sunday, December 24, 1989*

In my bedroom, I stood before the full-length mirror, waiting for Nigel to pick me up. *Rudolph the Red-Nosed Reindeer* blared from the TV in the other room. It was my sister's favorite.

I examined myself from head to toe. My hair was still short, but a lot longer than it had been. With my bright red oversized sweater and a white miniskirt, I looked festive. Anything to help put me in the holiday spirit. My appearance surprised me. I felt this was my way of reinventing myself. This was yet another Tatum. This was a Tatum that didn't have the stressors of a Mob family demanding her commitment. Didn't have to worry about speaking for anyone or anything. Who needed that shit? Not me. Zach was marrying someone else, and it was time to move on. I would allow myself to be happy.

I glanced over at the picture of my grandparents on their last wedding anniversary together. "Grandma, I feel back on track. Nigel's good to me. Real good. I'm moving on. You were right, Zach is a package deal, and I don't want the whole package. He is his family."

I reached for the frame and kissed the picture. "Love and miss you. Merry Christmas."

"Tatum, uh, Nigel's here," my mom called from the living room.

Showtime. I walked around the corner, and Toni was harassing the sexy James Dean lookalike. Nigel wore a black peacoat, with his typical blue jeans exposing his boots.

Toni had her tiny hands on her hips, looking up at Nigel, laughing. "You look old. What number are you?"

This was the first time my family had been home when Nigel picked me up. Nigel had always taken me out on a weekend night after my parents were already gone. I felt bad putting him on the spot.

Mom grabbed Toni and placed her on the couch. "That is not how we talk to our guests, young lady."

"Hi, Nigel," I said, making my presence known.

Mom looked at me and stood up all the way, heading in my direction. She whispered, "She's right. How old is he?"

I stepped away from her. "So, Nigel, I take it you've met my mom and sister?"

I walked over to him and took his scent in, expensive fresh sandalwood. Better known as heaven.

"Yes. Thank you again, Mrs. Duncan, for allowing Tatum to spend the holiday with us. What time should I have her home?"

I looked back at my mom with a raised eyebrow. I knew she was crapping her pants for how polite he was. "Well, Mom?" I wanted to laugh out loud. Not that Zach wasn't polite, there was just something different about Nigel's manners. With Zach, you knew he was asking to be nice, but he'd do what he wanted. With Nigel, he was sincere. Maybe it was the English accent.

"Eleven would be fine." Mom looked down at Toni. "Santa still has to come tonight. Right, Toni?"

Toni jumped to her feet. "Hurry, Tatey, and get back home so Santa can come!"

I stepped over to Toni and gave her a hug. "Okay, Tone. Get to bed before I do."

She hugged back and then jumped down, running off. "I tell Daddy to get ready for bed. Santa's coming."

I laughed, "I think 'Santa' is well aware of that."

Down the driveway, Nigel got the car door for me and we drove off in the big Mercedes S-Class. Within a few short minutes, my butt was toasty. I glanced down to the console and saw two small red dots lit up.

Nigel glanced at me. "Is it too hot? You can turn it down to low if you'd like."

I flipped the switch, and one red light stayed bright. Hot damn, this was a nice car. Zach's old Camaro didn't do that. For a split second my chest ached, but screw that. I had to remember that Zach had abandoned me. You don't abandon who and what you love. You fight for it.

"I'm nervous to meet your family, Nigel."

He didn't take his eyes off the road. "Oi, what? Nah . . . they're easygoin'. Nothing to worry about." With a big smile on his face, he reached over and grabbed my hand. "They're goin' to love you." He turned toward me for a split second. His eyes gave me that look again. "Don't be nervous, be yourself."

I was still nervous. Nigel tried to make me feel better, but instead I think he calmed himself.

A short ten-minute drive, and we reached a road that

was narrow and winding. You couldn't see around the corners. The roads were pretty with trees lining them, but my concern was an animal jumping out in front of us. We wouldn't see it coming. A few tight corners later and we turned down a private road in a wooded area. I couldn't wait to get there. Holding my breath around every corner wasn't the best way to calm my nerves. And the snow flurries weren't ideal conditions for those tight corners.

"Here we are. Brilliant, everyone is here."

What did Nigel mean by 'everyone'? "Um, just how many people am I meeting?"

Nigel laughed. "Just a few. You'll be fine."

He put the car in park and tapped my knee, and then ran around to open my car door. He put his hand out. "Here . . . don't slip."

After I stepped away from the car and he shut the door behind me, I looked up at the sky. It was beautiful. The evergreens circling his house had a few flakes on them. The snow was sticking. "Nigel, the house is beautiful."

It was a Southern-style mansion with beautiful landscape around the property. Christmas lights decorated the large white pillars in front. A life-sized Santa sat swinging on the wraparound porch. It was cheerful. And maybe just what I needed. "My goodness . . . someone here likes Christmas."

Nigel walked me up to his house. To say I was slightly intimidated would have been a huge misrepresentation. He flung open the double-wide front doors, and I breathed in an intoxicating orange, rosemary and cinnamon fragrance. It was wonderful.

I stepped inside, taking a deep breath. Something had me hesitant. It was the fact that I had never met

Zach's family in the month we were dating. I wasn't even dating Nigel, and I was meeting his family . . . at Christmas. Of course, Nigel and I had been seeing each other for three weeks now. I supposed it wasn't that far off.

Two women shorter than I was came rushing toward us. A few burly men stayed back, holding cocktails and grinning as they watched.

Nigel smiled and stepped sideways, "Mum, Aunt Sally . . . this is Tatum. Tatum, this is my mum, Mrs. Marshall. And my Aunt Sally, Mrs. Holmes."

I put my hand out, but they bypassed my hand and grabbed me. "Merry Christmas, Tatum. So nice to finally meet you."

They backed up. Both women had graying blond hair. Nigel's mom had long hair, and his Aunt Sally had short hair. A few wrinkles and makeup made up the difference between the women. Nigel's mom dressed a bit more stylishly than his aunt, who was dressed more casually.

Nigel took my coat and purse. His mother took my hand and walked me back into the house, down the hall to where the men stood.

"Guys, this is Tatum, Nigel's new girlfriend."

I choked on my own saliva and had to beat on my chest. Who said I was Nigel's girlfriend?

"Oh, sweetheart, are you okay?" Mrs. Marshall, Nigel's mom, asked.

Nigel came rushing up behind me, grabbing my waist with one hand while the other hand patted my back. "Um, no, Mum, she's just a friend."

A young woman walked in the room holding a glass of wine. "Geez, Mum. Let the poor girl meet his family first. That's later tonight."

I had to examine this girl. She resembled Nigel, but older. Maybe in her early twenties.

"Shut it, Bren. Just keep the glass up to that trap of yours." Nigel snickered.

I cleared my throat. "I'm sorry. Went down the wrong pipe."

Bren laughed as she sat on a bar stool up at their granite wraparound kitchen counter. Everything was big in the house. "Tatum, you should be pissed that your 'friend' here let you walk into this fiasco."

One of the taller gentlemen stepped up to her and they tapped bar glasses. "You said it, kiddo." He had a Southern accent.

Nigel looked at me. "Tatum, that's my sister, Bren. Stay away from her, she's an ass."

I began choking again. *What did I walk into?*

Evidently they all found the exchanges funny. I was the only one who appeared confused.

Nigel pointed to the man who'd spoken with the heavy drawl. "My stepdad, Lester. He's from the South, so just ignore any foolishness."

Lester stuck his tongue out at Nigel. I was shocked by how they teased the hell out of each other, and that was fine. British humor? No. Lester was from the South.

"Then my grandpa, Oscar."

Grandpa Oscar was a gentle-looking old man, sipping his cocktail in an old-fashioned glass. I recognized the barware because my grandmother had some similar glasses. I stepped up to him and put my hand out. "Nice to meet you. Merry Christmas, Grandpa Oscar."

He shook my hand and smiled ear to ear, looking around at his family. "She's staying, I like her." He turned around and found the recliner by the fireplace.

"And this is my Uncle Ted. He married Sally."

We all shared pleasantries and they dispersed. Nigel took my hand and whispered, "Happy Christmas, Tatum. Let me give you a tour."

Everything in their home had a story. At times, a sad story. Like the only family heirloom, a vase that had survived the bombing of London during World War II. I found their home so rich in culture and love, I couldn't help but want to stay.

Christmas music was playing softly around the house. Nigel and I made our way to the backyard once we finished the inside. I found myself at peace, standing on their back terrace, watching the snow flurries blow around in the light wind. The only word I could have used to describe how I felt at Nigel's home: magical. Acre upon acre filled with trees. And it was beautiful with the snow. Nothing to sled in, but just enough to show the white.

"Tatum, are you okay?"

Nigel strolled up next me, so close his warmth radiated onto my skin. He was so handsome. His sparkling blue eyes matched the Christmas lights they had around the property. "I couldn't be better. Thank you for having me."

I saw a deer out in the distance watching us. I focused to make sure it was really there.

"They come out all the time. Lester feeds them."

"You feed the deer here? That's wonderful."

Nigel chuckled. "Did you think we'd shoot them?"

"Not everyone thinks like that, Nigel."

"We do."

His beautiful blues, lined with jet-black eyelashes, mesmerized my soul.

This was too good to be true. I wasn't a lucky person. Then I had to ruin the one good thing in my life with irrational thoughts. Nigel would eventually leave me. I couldn't get close to him.

I backed away from the edge of the porch, forcing any happiness under my boot. "I'm cold."

"Wait, be right back," Nigel yelled as he ran inside.

Seconds later he came running out of the house with our coats draped over one arm and a thick wool blanket in the other. "Here, put this on. I want to take you out there."

"Out in the woods?" I glanced back to the overwhelming land with a thick forest just past the yard line. It didn't appear to be too dark. Actually, it was bright and glowing with the snow and Christmas lights.

He draped the wool blanket around me and took my hand. With my other hand, I held the blanket closed. With our coats on, Nigel and I walked out onto their perfectly manicured property.

Our fingers locked together, and my hand was warmed. It dawned on me that this was the first time since my grandma had died that I felt at complete ease. Nigel made me feel safe. Nigel made me happy.

The deer ran off as we got closer.

"Nigel, we probably shouldn't disturb them."

"They're used to us." He looked at me with the most mesmerizing grin. I didn't need my grandma guiding me to see his eyes were true. He was an honest person. He was gentle. He liked me.

I caught myself smiling back.

We stopped at the edge of the trees, and he faced me. "I hope I'm not wrong about this, otherwise . . ." he glanced up at the house and then back at me.

I wasn't sure what he was doing. I looked at the

house too.

Nigel came back to me and exhaled, but didn't say anything. I opened my blanket. "Nigel, here. The wind is picking up."

He took a breath and accepted my invitation to join me in the blanket. The moment I wrapped it around his shoulders, I knew where this was going. We felt so good together, an immediate ache in my chest told me I couldn't ignore what happened when I was this close to Nigel. There was something about him I found irresistible. It was more than feeling safe.

Nigel put his nose close to mine.

"Nigel, what is it?"

His eyes drooped. That look was back. "Tatum, I really want to be with you. I know this is moving too fast . . . we both have some baggage." His eyes brightened and pierced mine. "Go out with me?"

Go out with him? Steady? Thank god he didn't ask me to speak for him. But then again, Nigel was a normal guy. With a normal family. A *normal* grandpa. "Steady?"

"If you want. I know you're trying to move on . . . do we need a title?"

Hell, no. I hated titles. "Well, you have been the only guy I've seen since he left. I love spending time with you. I'm sure that's no secret."

Nigel brushed my bangs away from my face with a soft stroke. Then he slowly took the back of his finger down my jawline. "You're so beautiful, Tatum."

That gentle stroke sent zing after zing up my spine. Throwing all reservation to the wind, I reached up to his face and kissed his warm lips. Exactly what I wanted. Exactly what I missed.

Nigel grabbed me and squeezed my body into his.

His chest pulsated faster than mine. Another charge sprang up my back. Nigel was taking me on our first kiss ride. And damn it if my body didn't want more. It sprinted past my thought process and demanded control, throwing logic out the window. Nigel's kisses were wickedly good.

Nigel and I could have been standing next to their fireplace, because I only felt warmth.

My chest reacted. This was moving fast. It scared me how little reservation I had, if any. I pulled back and so did Nigel.

"Yes," I breathed. "I'll go out with you. Under one condition: always be honest and up front with me. Please."

"That's it?" His eyes narrowed, but he bit his lip, as if they ached to be touched again.

"You know what I mean."

He nodded. "Of course, m'lady."

I couldn't help but pull the dog head tilt. "'M'lady'?"

He chuckled, which looked adorable. "Sorry. Um . . . how to say . . ."

"How about just Tatum?"

His eyes changed, looking as wicked as his kisses. "Oh, Tatum, you are so much more than *just* Tatum. Surely not what you want to hear, but I understand why he's left town if it was over between you two."

"Huh? Who? Zach?"

"Yes. Being with you . . . there's this idea I get. Like seeing my future. You do this to me."

Nigel was right, he gave me a certain feeling too. And the feeling sure as hell wasn't fear.

Waking the morning of Christmas always made my heart race. No sooner had I smelled sugar cookies in the oven than Toni was running down the hall toward my bedroom.

"Tatey? Tatey? Get up. Santa came. Hurry." She busted through my door. "Mom won't let me touch nofing until you get here. Hurry." She pulled my door shut and ran off, still yelling about opening presents.

I stretched out and noticed Gizmo doing the same next to me. Lazy dog.

I walked over to my dresser and looked at the two garment boxes lying there. They brought a smile to my face. Nigel's Christmas gift to me was a sexy, sequined, long-sleeved dress. The hem came above my knees and it had a dramatically low backline. The dress hugged every curve. He requested I wear it for his New Year's party.

In the second box lay an awesome navy blue Guess blazer, nicely lined, that his parents gave me. When Mrs. Marshall had handed me the present last night, wrapped in metallic red paper, I hadn't known what to say.

I could still feel the high I was on from the previous night. It had been a perfect Christmas Eve. All thanks to Nigel and his family.

"Tatey?" Toni called.

Dressed and freshened up in record time, I hustled into the living room. Dad had Johnny Mathis Christmas music playing, and Mom had *A Christmas Story* on the TV in the background. It meant present time.

"So, Tatum, how did it go with Nigel's family last night?" Mom asked.

Toni was ripping wrapping paper off a present so

fast you could barely see her little hands.

"Great. His family was so nice, and they got me a present."

I was proud to show them my gifts. My parents would sneak a raised eyebrow at each other when they thought I wasn't paying attention. I still noticed. Their behavior told me they both were happy Nigel was in the picture and the Italian wasn't.

"And so you guys know . . . Nigel asked me to be his girlfriend."

My parents' eyes expanded. Mom glanced at my dad. "Oh, wow. So soon?"

"Yeah, but it's nothing too serious right now. We both just like each other and really don't want any labels. But I don't want you to think there's anyone else I'm interested in."

"Well, thank you for being so open and up front with us, Tatum. Your mother and I appreciate your honesty."

If I was starting over, then there must be a clean slate with everyone. Nigel was in my life to stay. "Sure. I just don't want you to think anything different. Because it wouldn't be true."

Mom nodded. "Yeah, we agree. This is for the best."

"So, would it be okay for him to stop by later this evening?"

My parents didn't mind. They acted as if they encouraged Nigel's presence.

Toni tossed a gift on my lap. "Here, Tatey. You're up."

Yeah. Maybe it was my turn to focus on what was best for me for a change? Maybe instead of looking at what I'd lost, I should look at what I'd gained. And gaining a wonderful, gentle, *normal* guy was the best gift possible.

## CHAPTER 21

**Zach**

*Tuesday, December 26, 1989*

The day after Christmas, and there I was, forced to be back at work. Standing in Davide's chilled wine cellar sucked. I didn't want to be anywhere near his family. Gramps had warned me during dinner that he had a meeting with Davide and wanted Vito, Tyler, and me to join him.

In the cellar, Tyler stood next to me, our hands behind our backs. Tyler didn't move. I wasn't sure if he was even breathing. Vito and Gramps sat in front of Davide's desk. Davide's men stood behind him.

If Tatum saw the meeting, she would never speak to me again. This was the kind of crap that scared the hell out of her, and I couldn't say I blamed her. All day I'd wondered how her Christmas had gone. Hopefully she was okay, since it was the first one since her grandma had died. The first of any holiday or celebration was the hardest.

"Zacharia? Zacharia?" Gramps growled.

I shook my head, leaving a deep thought, and

noticed Gramps was turned around in his chair. "I talking to you."

"Sorry, Gramps. How can I help?" At times like this Gramps should have spoken Italian, he knew his English was poor. But I supposed showing off to Davide was more important.

Evidently Tyler was breathing because he exhaled, and Uncle Vito didn't look my way. Shit. How long did he call my name and I didn't answer him?

"Your time has been requested by Mariacella."

The cellar was no longer cool. I could feel a heated wetness around my shirt collar. "Of course." I turned my attention. "Davide, I would love to spend time with your daughter. Whatever she'd like to do. I will be honored to treat her."

The old timer puffed on his cigar. "Excellent. You call her tonight and make arrangements. She very pleased to hear about you visit."

I nodded. Nothing more. They wouldn't get anything else out of me. Or I'll be damned to hell.

"It's no visit, Davide," Gramps said, turning back around. "He's living with Vito." Gramps barely moved his head back in my direction, but I could sense his eyes warning me not to say a word in defiance.

"Mariacella will be most pleased to hear. So everything in the States is set."

Now I was paranoid. Was Davide referring to Sergio's mess, or my spoken for?

"Yes. Everything is exactly where I want it. There will be no further delay," Gramps said.

"Excellent. Excellent. My girl, she's so crazy over your grandson." Davide laughed.

Great. They were referring to Tatum. How long had Gramps had this planned, to marry me off to this family? Out of all of the daughters Gramps could have hooked me up with, it had to be Mariacella. She was more than boy crazy. She was a whore. The problem with this family was that Davide had one child and she was spoiled rotten. He wasn't a complete idiot, though. He knew it was best to find someone who could take over his empire when the time came. He knew what had taken him over a half-century to build, she'd ruin within a month.

Returning to Bertano Manor, Uncle Vito couldn't pull down their cobblestone driveway fast enough. I wanted out of the car and away from Gramps.

Gramps sat in the passenger seat, proud of how the meeting with Davide had gone. "Once Zacharia marries into Davide's family, they'll get extra security from us, and his territory won't shrink anymore. He will be taken care of. And we . . . we get more power and money. Enough to make sure my family is taken care of for generations. We talk with the others as soon as we get in."

"Yes, Gramps," Vito replied.

Vito parked the Mercedes, and we followed Gramps inside the manor.

In the hall, I called out, "Gramps, is there anything else?"

Gramps waved his hand, never looking back at me. "Not now. Call Mariacella soon." Gramps continued to walk into Vito's office. "Vito, get the others, we need to discuss the next move."

Vito glanced back at me. His eyes spoke sympathy, but never faltering strength. "Of course, Gramps, right away."

Tyler stood next to me in the hall. The doorway next to us led to the pool house. He grabbed my arm and tugged me inside.

Matt and Bobby were in the pool and quieted once they noticed we were in there.

I walked over to the patio table near the pool.

"Zach, we need a plan."

I took a chair. Matt and Bob got out of the water, heading in my direction. "I already have one."

Tyler sat next to me. "What? And don't say getting drunk. You've been drinking too much recently. Getting drunk and stoned isn't the way to cope with this."

Bobby and Matt joined us at the table.

"No. But will you drive me to Frankie's?"

"The tattoo parlor?"

"Yeah, that's the one."

---

Tyler drove me to Frankie's Tattoo Parlor. Bob and Matt insisted on going with us. Frankie was the artist who did all of the tattoos for my family who lived in Italy. I relaxed in his big, black leather chair. Frankie had the chair tilted back a little and the side arm rails moved out, away from my body. My forearms, facing upward, rested out at an angle on the cushioned leather armrests.

He worked on the inside of my left forearm first. "So does your Gramps even like this German girl of yours? What's so bad about her?"

It didn't worry me to talk about Tatum with Frankie. After he finished my forearms, there would be no hiding my feelings for my spoken for anyway. "Nothing. There's nothing wrong with her. And the strange thing is, they're similar. Both Gramps and

Tatum are pigheaded, determined people."

"Yeah, Gramps can be pigheaded." Frankie laughed.

"But it doesn't matter what he says, she's on me now. Forever."

My cousins stood there watching as Frankie inked my forearms. They would give an occasional glance at each other, but they never said a word. Not one. They knew better.

After we left Frankie's parlor, I had to get ready for my "date" with Mariacella. Of course, once I'd called her, she'd insisted we meet up right away.

Back at Bertano Manor, I stood in the bathroom, examining myself in the long mirror. I had on a black long-sleeved button-down shirt with the sleeves rolled up so you could just barely see "Tatum" on my arms. My arms had protective ointment on since the fresh tattoos were exposed. I wondered what everyone else in the family would say when they saw my new ink. It didn't matter, they weren't coming off.

Someone knocked on the door. "Zacharia, it's Mom."

"Come in."

She stepped inside as I walked out of the bathroom. I would do my best not to worry her. Ever. She and dad had been great trying to get Gramps to reconsider, but they'd only achieved failure.

She immediately looked at my forearms. "Zacharia, we know you're hurting, and god knows if I could take that pain from you I would."

"I hate this. You know Mariacella isn't the cute little girl we played with as kids when we'd visit. She's a whore, Mom. She'll fuck anything she wants. And I have to 'entertain' her. No. No one can help me, and that's the fucking problem," I stepped past her and grabbed my wallet Gramps had filled with 500,000 lire—about 500 dollars—off the bed and tucked it in my black slacks.

"You heard Gramps warn me just an hour ago not to let him down. I'm the missing link for this deal. *I'm*"—I pointed to my chest—"to keep her happy."

She grabbed my shoulders and forced me to face her. "They're moving forward with you taking over when the time comes. I know you don't want to, but it sounds like keeping her happy for now is working. If you can take—"

"Do you not hear yourself, Mom? Keeping her happy is our goal?"

"I know. But if we keep *all* of them happy, maybe we'll have grounds for renegotiating your return home. Zacharia, I want my boy home with me. Not here under Davide's control."

I pulled away. "Yeah, well . . . did you know Gramps also had Bobby seal the deal with Tatum before you guys left St. Louis?" The look on her face gave me the answer. "You're a Lead, you should have been told."

"What did Gramps have him do, Zacharia?"

I glanced at the intercom to make sure no one was listening in. The lights were all off, so we were alone. "He had Bobby tell her I was marrying someone else."

Mom gasped, covering her mouth. Her eyes became glassy.

"The old man told Bobby to make sure Tatum knew they were prepping me to marry an Italian girl, that's why I'm here. That's why I'm living in Italy now."

"Oh my god, he didn't?"

"He did. I thought we were trying to get out of this lifestyle? Mom, you know Gramps is pulling us in further with this deal."

She hugged me to her chest. "Oh, Zacharia. I'm so sorry." Mom backed away, but still held my shoulders. "I know. And so does your father. We've all talked about it recently. Sergio. Piero. And even Vito. None of the Leads want this deal to happen. But if Gramps says so, they'll abide by it. We all have to. But tell me . . . how do you know for sure about Baldassario and Gramps?"

All of the Elders called us by our Italian names in Italy. "I overheard Gramps talking to Bobby about it after you guys arrived the other night. Don't worry, they had no clue I was even there."

"Zacharia, I swear your father and I had no clue about this, or we would have tried to stop it. That poor girl doesn't need anything else to worry about either."

"I know. And I'm sure Bobby only did it because the orders came from Gramps."

"You haven't said anything to Baldassario?"

"Nah. Bobby is in the middle enough as it is. Why make it harder on him?"

"Oh, son . . ." Mom exhaled. "All right. Just get this over with. Then when we all leave after the New Year, you'll be on the plane with us. I promise you that." Mom grabbed me in a bear hug. "Zacharia. I know this hurts, but let's just stay focused on getting you home with us. Okay?"

I couldn't look at her. Her tears made me think of Tatum, and how she probably felt when Bobby told her about Mariacella. None of it mattered. I couldn't do anything about Tatum until I got back to St. Louis. For now, I had to do what I could to make this deal happen between Davide and Gramps.

"Yeah. I'll do whatever it takes to get to Tatum."

I drove up to Davide's front gate, and a guard came out of their security post. "Do you have an appointment?"

"I do, with Mariacella. Please tell her Zacharia is here." I hated using my Italian name. Tatum would use it when she was pissed. But as much crap as I gave her for calling me Zachy, I preferred it. This was not the time to laugh about her American manners, though.

*Damn it to hell. Stop thinking about her.*

I glanced at my forearms. Seeing her name on my skin made me feel closer to her. And yet, I had to push her so far away to do this.

## CHAPTER 22

**Zach**

After a long, dragged-out dinner at the most expensive restaurant in Bologna, I drove Mariacella back to her estate. We pulled up to their eighteen-foot-tall, ornate black gate.

The guard stepped out of his booth and bent down to look in the car. He saw Mariacella and said, "Your father got tired of waiting for you. He said he'd talk to you in the morning to see how it went."

She winked. "Thanks."

He opened the gate, and I drove up to the estate's main entrance. Bertano Manor was an anthill compared to the size of her father's estate, so how it was dwindling down, I had no clue. I had to think there was another reason Gramps wanted to take over, other than money and power. He was never hungry for those before. And they wanted me to take this enterprise over when the time came? No way in hell.

"Zacharia, take the right drive. We can go in my entrance and not disturb the rest of the house."

"Of course." I wondered how many other guys she said that to.

Moments later, we stepped into Mariacella's bedroom. Like she said, the whole wing was hers. Davide was nowhere near. Neither was anyone else, for that matter.

Mariacella's bedroom was right out of a princess fairytale magazine. Ice-pink velvet fabric was pinned around the walls, and white crown molding decorated the room. She walked over to her white wood sleigh bed covered in soft pink linens. Tatum's room wasn't this girly.

Then I spotted a fully stocked silver bar cart. "Mariacella, you want a drink? I'm pouring myself one." I didn't ask. It was there for a reason. And god knew I needed a damn drink if I was going to be anywhere near Princess.

"Oh Zacharia, you take such good care of me—"

"Do you want a drink or not?"

"Touchy. Touchy. Touchy. Except with me . . . yes, I will. Grazie."

I made her drink stiff, real stiff. Maybe if she passed out, I could leave. "Here you go, drink up."

"Salute." She threw it back. Impressive, considering it was straight vodka.

"Salute." Then I tossed mine back.

"Zacharia, come." She patted the bed. "Join me."

"You know . . . that pink chair by the window there looks pretty comfy. Let me try that out first."

She leaped out of bed and stood before me in front of the chair. "You so sexy. This is the perfect spot to start."

I took her arms and gently guided her back to the bed, avoiding any glances at the sizable cleavage from her low-cut sweater. "How about we talk first and have a few drinks."

She took the edge of the bed for now and I went back to the damn pink chair.

"You're too funny. About what?"

"To just talk, Mariacella, is not funny. So—" I swallowed the lump in my throat and wiped my forehead dry. "Are you going to college starting in the fall?"

Mariacella pulled off her sweater, exposing a thin cami underneath. She rolled onto her stomach and faced me, her boobs nearly popping out of the top.

"I'm traveling. School can come later." Her accent was almost worse than her father's.

Why she and her father insisted on speaking English with me was insulting. All of the Bertanos knew Italian. "Cool. Traveling is good. Friends? Boyfriends?"

Mariacella's face looked as if she'd bit into a sour grape. "No boyfriends. I take what I want, when I want. Besides, I prefer to travel with girls."

"Well, I have a girlfriend back in the States."

"No. I heard she not speak for you."

I could feel my chest burn. "You heard wrong. It doesn't matter." I walked over and poured another drink. "Mariacella, another?"

"Oh, you trying to get me drunk." She giggled, slurring her words.

At dinner, she'd had the whole bottle of wine by herself. This could work. Maybe she would pass out and this could end before it began. "Nope, you drink what you want. Yes or no?"

"Of course I will."

I handed her a serving, which was exactly two tequila shots. I went back to the pink escape pad. "I'm going to be honest with you, Mariacella."

She sat up to her knees, wiggling her ass like a dog

waiting for a treat.

"I'm not sure this is what you want."

"Ohh, that's so sweet." She was so drunk, her words were barely clear.

Great. If only she would pass out. "Sorry?"

Mariacella got off the bed and stood before me again. Of course putting her boobs back in my face. "I'll tell no one what happens tonight. It'll be our little secret. I want you more than anything." She swayed.

*Oh God, please just make her pass out, just do this one fucking favor.* I put her back on the bed before she fell over. If she woke with a knot on her head, it would be my head instead.

"Here, why don't you rest?"

I took the rose-petal sheet and pulled it up over her. Mariacella grabbed my shoulder. "Come in with me. I need you, Zacharia. Now."

"Mariacella, you've had a bit too much to drink. Are you sure?"

"Oh, such gentlemen. Now, join me."

"All right, but first I need your toilet."

"Out there. Go to right. Hurry."

"Thanks, I'll be back." Maybe by the time I got back, she'd be passed out cold.

Her bathroom matched her bedroom. So much pink I wanted to vomit.

I stood at the white marble vanity, hands locked on the edge, glaring at myself in the mirror. *Just fucking do it. Stop stalling. She's your one-way ticket back home. Do whatever she wants to keep her happy—then keeping Davide happy—then keeping Gramps happy— equals my return to Tatum. That's all that matters. Focus on the prize, Zach. Nothing else.*

Gramps's instructions before I left kept running

through my head. *"Zacharia, we're counting on you. You're the last link to this deal. If she tells her father how much she loves you and what a good time she had, we'll . . . I mean, you will inherit his enterprise. This means everything to me right now. You do whatever she wants to keep her happy. Don't fuck this up for us. Or else."*

Why did Gramps want this so bad? It didn't matter.

A few minutes later, I stepped back in her bedroom. Mariacella was spread out on her bed wearing dental floss. Her sheer black negligee showed off her assets. I made sure her door locked behind me. No going back.

The moment the lock clicked, she grabbed my arms and pulled me to bed. She was strong, or I was just weak. Or maybe I did too much. I landed on top of her.

"Oh, Zacharia, I've waited for such a long time to be with you." Mariacella forced me upright, causing me to straddle her.

She unbuttoned the top of my shirt. "I'll undress you." She stared at me, examining my face. "Zach, what did you do in the bathroom? Cocaine? Your eyes is bloodshot. And you have something white . . ." She reached up toward my face.

I jerked away. "No. I didn't do coke." I swiped the back of my hand across my nose. "Look, I don't have any condoms on me."

She popped up from her pillow and reached over to her nightstand and pulled open the drawer. Every color of the rainbow was represented. She had so many condoms in the drawer you couldn't see the bottom. She grabbed a gold one. "Here, use this."

I needed one last drink first. I reached for the last cocktail I'd made for her—she hadn't finished it—and threw it back.

Whoa. That burned. I had forgotten I'd given her straight tequila. I reached over to put the glass back on the nightstand.

"Come on, Bertano. Show me what your American girlfriend is missing."

As I pulled my hand away from the glass, my other hand went flying back. At the same time, I said, "What did you say?"

The back of my hand made contact. I didn't mean to. I didn't even aim, but my hand met Mariacella's cheek. *Fuck.* "Mariacella, oh my god . . . I'm so sorry. I flinched."

For a second she was shocked, holding her cheek. But her eyes relaxed and she laughed. "Oh, you do like it rough. Good. I do too."

Of course she liked it rough. But why should I complain? She wasn't mad. I could breathe again. What caused me to react like that? I could keep my cool with girls. Especially with a girl who had a very powerful father. Shit.

I took the condom she had dropped on her chest when she'd grabbed her cheek.

Her hands at my zipper caught my attention. "Whoa, let me do that."

"Finally." She took her hand and ran it along my face. "I so lonely. Stay the night with me."

Her cheek looked as if she had more blush on than needed. Damn it. I prayed the redness would be gone by morning.

Mariacella flopped back. "Relax, Zacharia. I take good care of you." She slid the negligee's straps off her shoulders, exposing her breasts.

*Just remember, Zach . . . this is your ticket home.*

Something hit me in the face. I jumped up, trying to focus in the dimly lit room, and as I did, an arm slid off me. I was in bed.

"Uhhh," Mariacella moaned. She was asleep, but rolled away from me.

Jesus. I had to get out of her bedroom before her father found me. Then again, they'd probably be happy, thinking a wedding would soon come. Over my dead body.

This was not the time to be loud and clunky. I had to get out and quick. First things first, I had to find my clothes. Shit. Things really had gotten out of hand. My clothes were thrown all over her room. Within minutes, I had her room put back in order and my clothes on, and I'd eliminated every sign I was ever there.

From her bedroom window, it was a short drop down to my car. A quiet escape was the only way. I didn't need to run into her father. I snuck out her window, closing it behind me, and jumped. I made sure to casually wave goodbye to the gate guard as I drove past. I made it. I was out.

When I pulled into Bertano Manor's garage, my dad was in there waiting. I didn't give him a second glance. He looked tired.

I stepped out of the car and walked in his direction. "Dad, what are you doing up? It's like—" I looked at my watch. "It's four am."

Dad didn't say a word. Not that that was alarming, but it definitely wasn't typical.

He stepped up to me and threw his arms around me. "I'm sorry, my son."

I backed away. "Why?" We kept our voices down.

"Your mother and I couldn't prevent this."

"Dad, it's over. Just forget it."

Dad took a nasally breath in and glanced up at the ceiling. "What will Tatum do?" He looked at me. His eyes drooped and his lips tucked tight. Dad was afraid.

"Exactly what you think she'll do. Because she's loyal, she's predictable."

He turned around, running his hands through his hair. "After Mariacella's report reaches us, we're all getting Gramps to allow you to come home with us. He can't argue if everyone agrees and she's happy. Just let her think you're in love with her for now."

"Dad, she knows I'm not. I told her about my spoken for."

He didn't move. "Really? She knows about Tatum?"

"Yeah."

He lifted his head, breathing while looking out into the possibilities of what that would mean.

"She saw this too." I lifted my sleeves and showed Dad the tattoos.

Dad's eyes came to life. "Yes. Your mother told me about your visit to Frankie's. And Mariacella still wanted to slee . . . never mind. It's over. Let's just hope she only has good things to say about your date."

Crap. If her cheek was still red when she woke, who knew how she would recall the incident. "Dad, there's one thing that could come back."

I never realized how many times Dad took deep breaths. "Okay."

"I kind of backhanded her." Yup, not what my dad wanted to hear. "Look, it happened so fast and I swear it was an accident. Dad, you know I would never mean to hit a girl. Never. At the time she laughed about it, but I left before she got up, so I have no clue what it looks like. I just pray there's no mark today."

Dad had to breathe through his mouth. "Okay, so you smacked her becausssse . . .?"

"She said something about Tatum."

Dad's chest rose. "Zacharia, my god, why couldn't you ignore her?" He paced toward the wall, then back to me. "So what if she says Tatum's a bitch or whatever."

"You're right, I should have, but I didn't. I'm just telling you in case. She may not even remember it was me."

Dad glared at me. He knew it got wild with Mariacella. She wasn't one to have a nice, quiet and intimate experience. Her reputation was more than a girl who partied and easily slept with whoever was "fun" that night. My experience with her was no exception. It was shameful. No, it was disgusting. I would never treat the woman I loved like that. The shit she wanted from me. I could remember most of it. Some I was glad was lost because of the booze and drugs.

My stomach churned. I didn't feel well. The garage was moving. Or I was.

I ran for the garage restroom and threw up.

Dad came in behind me and patted my back after I flushed the toilet. "And in case you were wondering . . . I know. How long have you been taking that shit?"

I stood up and went for the sink to rinse and splash water on my face. "Since I got here."

"What the hell are you thinking, using that shit, Zacharia?" Dad's voice rose.

I dried off my hands and turned around to him. "I can't handle it here. With Gramps having me "entertain" Mariacella. The future marriage. Getting to know Davide's other Italian associates. I want out, and I will fucking kill Mariacella if I have to marry her. That's why. It makes it easier."

Dad pointed his finger at me. No telling what physical reaction he'd have if I weren't his son. "I don't give a fuck. We all have shit to deal with. A Bertano doesn't cope by using drugs, damn it. You're stronger than that. Get off that shit right now. Or else."

## CHAPTER 23

*Tatum*

*Saturday, December 30$^{th}$, 1989*

Nigel was taking me out for dinner. He didn't mention where, just said I should dress nicely. I wore a denim miniskirt with the new blazer his parents got me for Christmas.

"Where are you taking me?" I asked him.

Nigel didn't take his eyes off the road. He just smiled. "We're almost there. Can you wait a few more minutes?"

I didn't let Nigel know how much I enjoyed a good surprise. Didn't want him to think he could do this all the time. Surprises made me too anxious. But I did love them.

Minutes later, he pulled into the parking lot of my grandparents' favorite restaurant. "Nigel, what are we doing here?"

He parked the car and faced me, his knee on the seat. "Tomorrow is our one-week anniversary, but we have the party at my house. I want to celebrate early." He took a quick glance at the restaurant door. "I know this restaurant holds a lot of memories for you. I thought it would be a good idea for us. But if it's too much to handle, we can go elsewhere. I don't mind. It's your call."

I glanced up at the door too. It was exactly what I would like. If he was willing to keep a tradition in my family, why argue? I touched his knee. "This is perfect. I'm just surprised you listened to me the other night when I went on and on and on about them."

When I'd talked about them to Kyle, he would interrupt to talk about football strategies. Zach always listened, I was just careful with whom I talked to about my grandparents. Not everyone cared.

"Why would you think I didn't listen? I asked about the picture of them on your dresser. If I didn't want to know, I wouldn't have asked. Besides, whether I asked or not, I'd still listen, Tate."

Nigel clicked on the furnace with his ability to be sensitive, and he didn't even know it.

He leaned over and stole a kiss. "Since we're staying, let's go in. I'm hungry."

We walked into the restaurant and what do you know, the same hostess from all those years ago was there waiting for us. She looked at me and did a double take. "Oh my word . . . little Tatey Duncan! You're not so little anymore, now are you?"

For a second I was embarrassed by my nickname, but Nigel seemed to enjoy her reaction to seeing me.

"Hi, Mrs. Clark. How are you?"

"Oh, same old, same old. How's the family doing?"

"Just fine. Thanks."

Mrs. Clark placed her hand on my shoulder. "We all miss your grandparents, dear."

Nigel put his arm around my waist. I could only nod.

If a single word came out of my mouth, a tear would follow.

She shook off the last comment and stepped over to her appointment book. Looking up at Nigel, she smiled. "And I see you made reservations for two and it's a special dinner?"

"Yes. That's correct," Nigel answered.

Mrs. Clark smiled and asked us to follow her. She sat us at a private two-top table in a cozy corner. Besides the typical china and glassware, there was a small floral arrangement of a single stargazer with two red roses and baby's breath placed on the center of the table. I looked at Nigel.

He gave my shoulders a little tug.

"For me?"

"Who else?" Nigel whispered in response and chuckled.

Mrs. Clark placed the menus down. "Is this suitable?"

Nigel nodded. "Brilliant."

"Now, Tatey, your desserts are on us." She looked at Nigel. "Whatever you wish, it's on the house."

We took our seats and thanked her. After she walked off, I sat there for a moment, taking in the restaurant. Not much had changed in a year and a half. Maybe new artwork on the walls and fresh linens, but otherwise, exactly the way my family saw it last. This was the perfect example of bittersweet. It was sad knowing what family I had was gone, but too, being with Nigel here made me feel hope that one day I'd make my own family memories to cherish.

Nigel took my hand. "Tate?"

I took a deep breath and couldn't feel more at ease. "Yeah?"

"You okay?"

My heart became a blooming flower—expanding. Not only did he bring me to a restaurant that meant so much to me, he had my favorite flower on the table waiting—stargazer lily.

I patted his hand. "I'm better than okay, Nige. This is just perfect."

"Nige?"

"Sorry, but I like calling you Nige too."

He laughed and grabbed the menu. "Go for it."

The waitress walked over and introduced herself. Nigel and I placed our order and she soon walked away. Another staff member delivered water. We always got good service in this family restaurant.

"So, Tate. About the party tomorrow, you're sure your parents don't mind if you spend the night at my house?"

"Uhh, I have it squared away."

He raised his black eyebrows at me. "That's code for you lied to them."

I laughed. "No. Not really."

"Tell them the truth, Tate. Don't lie, please. Would it help if my mum calls yours?"

"No. Don't worry about it." I said it fast and with a slight ring. It wasn't until those words came spewing out what they meant to me. Zach's face popped in my head and how he used to say those words burnt my ears. I had to make sure to never say those words together ever again. I didn't want to be reminded of *him*.

"Tate? Hello, Tate?"

I blinked. "Sorry, thinking of something." I smiled at Nigel.

And by the look on his face, he was thinking about something too. The lies coming out of my mouth.

"Okay, you win. I'll tell my parents the truth."

"There's no need to hide. My mum will be stopping in all night. Everyone who comes to the party is staying at the house. And my sister Bren will be there. Of course, not sure how much she can be trusted." He laughed.

"I'll take care of it, Nige. I promise."

"Okay, you better. I don't want your parents to think I had you lie to them."

Our salads were served. They, too, were exactly how I remembered them. "This looks so good. They have the best *Italian* dressing." Damn it. Why did I say that?

"I can't wait to try it."

I began cutting my salad in equal bites, whereas Nigel dug right in. Which meant he got to enjoy the salad sooner than I had.

"Hmm, this is good."

"I told ya."

"So, do you mind if I ask how often your family came here?"

I finally took my first bite. "No, that's fine. I like talking about them. We came for most holidays and birthdays, anniversaries . . . anything we had an excuse for."

I sat there staring at Nigel. He wasn't eating, just watching me. His lips were perfect. They reminded me of our first kiss. A wicked kiss. His eyes were soft and relaxed, but thinking. He was damn sexy. "What?"

"Nothing, just listening to you. I know how you feel. I like going to my dad's house. The house we're going to tomorrow. It has the furniture from my parents' pad when they lived in Surrey."

"I know you told me before, but when did he . . . you know?" I asked.

"I was four when he died. But we didn't move here until I was twelve."

"Oh, you were young, Nigel."

"Yeah. My grandma, his mum, she died the year before we moved here. She was the last of any relatives on my father's side."

"That's a small family. My grandma came from a big German Catholic family. In the past few years, though, it's not been good. It's like when one goes, they all start going."

"I know what you mean. So your family . . . they're German?"

"Mostly, German and Scots, on both sides. How about you?" For the love of god, I prayed he didn't say Italian.

"Mostly English and German."

I could feel my lips spread wide with the biggest smile. I exhaled, not sure why I'd held my breath.

After dinner, we were stuffed, but Nigel insisted we at least share a dessert since we were celebrating our anniversary and it was on the house.

The New York style cheesecake drizzled in cherry sauce was decorated with pristine red swirls. Nigel and I each held a fork but didn't know where to begin. The dessert was artwork.

"Ladies first."

Taking a modest bite and letting the cheesecake melt in my mouth, I said, "Oh my gosh . . . that is so good."

Nigel followed and reacted the same. "Good call on the cheesecake. What other desserts do you like?"

"Carrot cake. German Chocolate cake. But no pies. I'm not much of a pie fan. Cherry pie might be okay."

He laughed. "I've not met many people from the Midwest who don't love pies."

"Then you haven't met the right people, Nigel." I snickered.

I glanced up at him while letting another bite melt in my mouth. He had that look. I turned away, swiping my sweaty hands on my skirt. Something inside me changed. A different breed of butterfly fluttered around in my stomach. It was the first time I felt anxious around him. And I knew damn well why.

When Nigel drove me home, we sat in the car to finish making plans for the party.

"Okay, you're picking me up at five?"

"Yes, and don't wear the dress I got you, but bring it. Honestly, not sure how comfortable it will be wearing all night. The sequins may bother you. So you can put it on right before the party."

What guy thinks like that? Nigel. That's who. "Do you know how sweet you are?"

Nigel kept his stare out the front windshield, but smiled. Moments later he turned to me. "Tatum, why do you say that?"

"Not many guys would care, or take it into consideration, if it meant seeing a girl in a skintight dress."

"I'm not many guys."

With his accent on top of that, it was too much to handle. Nigel got that look. He leaned over to my seat, wove his fingers through the hair at the back of my head and drew my face to his. His kisses were more explosive than a Fourth of July fireworks finale. In the privacy of his car with dark tinted windows, I wasn't afraid. I wanted to feel him.

I went over to his lap. He put his hand down the side of the door, and his seat smoothly moved backward.

Nigel put his hands up to my face and cradled my cheeks. "Tatum, you are so beautiful."

I placed my hands on his headrest, and immediately recalled the last time I was in a similar position. Besides the obvious—being with a different guy—the most important difference was I didn't fear continuing a relationship with Nigel. I didn't fear where Nigel and I could take it.

I bent down to his handsome face and kissed his lips.

Within seconds, Nigel's body reacted, a sure sign it had to stop there.

I sat up. "Goodnight, Nigel. Thanks for a beautiful evening."

He wrapped his arms around me and flopped his head on my chest. "Oh, m'lady . . ."

"Oh just Tatum will be fine."

He backed away and laughed. "No. I said you're much more."

Nigel gave me one last kiss for the night.

## CHAPTER 24

*Tatum*

Sunday. December 31, 1989

The next morning, I had to get to the mall before the stores closed. Andi, Diane, and I all took the last-minute shopping trip for Nigel's New Year's Eve party.

Andi was looking forward to it. With Matt gone for the holidays, it wasn't easy on her. She got lonely. I was more than happy to have her join me at the party. I also didn't mind if she went back and let it slip how great Nigel was to me. It wouldn't bother me if the word got out. Accidentally.

And Diane, she was too fun to leave out. If I was going to meet a lot of Nigel's other friends, I needed a couple of mine with me.

Diane picked me and Andi up and drove us out to Jamestown Mall. Diane and I knew this mall better than the back of our hands. We wouldn't be long. That was, until Andi decided to get a new dress. I only needed sticky cups for my sequin dress—because of the dropped back I couldn't wear a bra. Diane wanted hosiery. Andi was going along for the ride until she saw that perfect strapless blue sequined dress.

"Look, Tate, we can kind of match. Sequins and sequins."

Andi tried on the sexy dress and my first thought was, *Matt would not want you wearing that thing without him there.* "Yup, I think you should totally get it."

An hour and a half later we'd found everything we needed, or wanted. That meant we'd worked up an appetite. "Let's stop in the restaurant and grab a quick bite before they close."

Diane adjusted her purse over her shoulder. "Good idea, Tate. I'm not sure when I'll eat next. And if we're drinking, we better eat something."

"Diane, who said anything about drinking?" I couldn't believe that had come out of her mouth.

Diane stopped in the middle of the mall and rolled her eyes at me. "Dear god, Tate. It's New Year's Eve, there will be alcohol."

Andi said nothing, but her face looked as if I'd asked her to get on the most insane roller coaster at Six Flags. She'd never drunk before either.

"You know Nigel's sister will be there and his mom will be coming and going all night, right?"

"Yeah, and I'm at a disco, but don't want to dance. Let's eat. I need to coat my stomach." Diane began walking again.

I was shocked to hear her speak about drinking in such a dismissive way. Andi agreed with me, giving doubtful looks behind Diane's back.

The restaurant hostess seated us in the corner booth, but in the front row, nearest to the mall. It was the perfect spot to people-watch as shoppers walked by.

We ordered as soon as the waitress came over.

Diane and I were eating our salads when something out in the mall caught Andi's attention. Andi ducked behind a plant on the half wall our booth butted up against.

Diane, who sat in the middle, looked out into the mall. "What is it, Andi?"

Andi played spy behind the plant. Her eyes got real big and she dropped down in the booth, grunting, "Tate, duck. It's Kyle."

Without thinking, I did as she said. All anyone ever had to do was say the magic word, Kyle, and I reacted. In the millisecond it took to say the name, my heart began beating out of my chest. This could not be happening here.

Seconds later Diane joined us, tucked below the table top. "Shit, I think he heard. Just stay down for a minute, he won't see us."

My heart jumped into a fifty-meter dash without any warm-up. I patted my chest. "He just won't give up. What's his problem? And damn it, Nigel isn't here."

I saw a bunch of legs walking up to our table. "Who the hell is Nigel?" Kyle's voice brought a pain to my entire body.

Andi and Diane looked at me. Both mouthed, "Sorry."

We sat up and noticed not only was Kyle there, but so were Bonnie and another guy from the football team. Three against three, but our three were much smaller.

"I heard Zach moved out of the country. Too bad."

"Tatum isn't talking to you, shithead," Andi said. It was an attempt to insult him, but Kyle only laughed.

"Ha. How about you and I have a chat outside, Tatum? I think the last time we met up, you had your boyfriend there. The one that left you. So about that chat."

Bonnie moved closer to our table. A smirk wider than our booth spread across her face. "Yeah, I've been waiting to get a piece of her ever since she told the entire school how loose my cheerleading skirts were."

Andi, Diane, and I all looked at each other and laughed. Bonnie was known, whether I said that or not, by the whole school to be the loose cheerleader.

"Tatum isn't going anywhere with you, asshole," Diane said.

Kyle laughed again. "What . . . you have your girlfriends doing the talking for you now? Get the fuck out of there, Tatum. I don't have all night." Kyle kept his voice down so the few restaurant customers couldn't hear him.

"I'm not going anywhere with you, psycho. You can leave now." If we stalled long enough for the waitress to come back over, we could get security's attention. I wished the mall was more crowded.

"That's interesting . . . because I'm not leaving without you." Kyle reached for my arm and pulled.

I couldn't move into the booth fast enough. Kyle got hold of my wrist. With that one move, the day from hell flashed before my eyes. *Kyle shoved me to the floor and sat on me, holding my wrists above my head. "You should've done this months ago. Now stop fighting me . . ."*

No. Kyle wouldn't hurt me again. I wouldn't allow it.

Bonnie and Kyle's other friend blocked Diane and Andi from getting out of the booth on the other side. They made it difficult for the restaurant side to see Kyle pulling on me.

Kyle ground his teeth and said, "I said, get your skinny ass outside."

"You let go of me right now or I'll scream," I said through gritted teeth. If only I could get my hand free.

"Drop m'lady. Now." Nigel. I heard Nigel's voice. What was he doing at the mall?

I looked around Kyle. He didn't let go, but straightened his back and turned his head. "Who the fuck are you?"

"I'm the guy that's going to break your nose if you don't take your filthy fucking hands off m'lady."

I could breathe again, even though they were deep, painful breaths. Nigel was here.

Kyle released my wrist and laughed. "So is Tatum screwing you now?"

Nigel put his hand out for me. I didn't think twice, I moved. Nigel pulled me to his side and quickly gave my lips a warm peck. He didn't say a word, only tilted his head behind him, nudging for me to get back.

He had two guys with him. They were both very tall. One had sandy-blond curly hair.

The other had brown hair longer than Willie Nelson's. He grabbed my shoulders and pulled me back behind Nigel, but next to him. "Sorry to meet you under these conditions, but I'm Jessie. Now don't move."

I didn't know what nightmare I'd fallen into.

"I'm sure no matter what Tatum is doing, or not doing, is none of your fucking business. What guy picks on a girl? You must have some major compensating to worry about."

Nigel hit a nerve, because Kyle's face was beet red. I glanced around the restaurant, and what few people were in there were watching. I wanted Kyle to get hauled away, but not all of us.

Kyle laughed. "Who the fuck . . . this is just great. One minute she's with a filthy Italian, the next a filthy Brit. Tatum, you are a slut."

All I heard was a low growl come from Nigel's chest, then Jessie pulled me backward, away from my boyfriend. Nigel reared back and his fist shot forward, meeting Kyle's face. There was a loud crack. Blood came pouring from Kyle's nose.

Nigel's blond friend grabbed napkins off the table and threw them at Kyle. "Oh man, that's a mess. Here." Blondie shoved Kyle away from us and toward the door. "You need to take that outside. You're making a mess, dude."

Kyle and the others hustled toward the mall door, blood soaking the napkins. Before they got outside the mall, security caught up to them. Someone must have called.

"Thanks, mate," Nigel said to his friend. He turned around and looked at me. His eyes were tiny. Definitely not the puppy dog face I was used to. Nigel put his arms up, and that was all it took.

I collided with his chest, tucking my head into him. "Oh my god, Nigel. Thank you. What are you doing here?"

"Mom asked me to pick something up for her from Dillard's. We walked by, and that's when I noticed it was you."

"Well, thank you." I looked up at him, "Not sure how that would have ended."

"Tatum, you'd call for help. You would have gotten up and made a scene—call for security. That's what would have happened."

"I would have been too afraid they would have called my parents too," I said, and looked away.

"Someone like that, you don't screw with, Tate. Any guy that would treat a girl like that, especially in public, is psychotic. You don't ever trust them, nor give them the chance. You hear me?"

I took a deep breath and nodded. I felt weak at the knees.

He squeezed me to him and kissed my lips. "How the hell do you know him?"

"Nigel, we need to take a seat or leave," Jessie said.

Nigel didn't let go while he pulled me back into the half-moon booth. Diane and Andi were followed by Nigel's friends on the other side.

I kept my voice down. "That's Kyle, Mr. Asshole Football Player at my school. I can't believe you broke his nose."

"I said I would. No one is going to lay a hand on you. But you and I have some talking to do, yeah?"

I nodded and tucked my head back on his chest. If it weren't for Nigel showing up when he did, god only knows what would have happened. I wouldn't let Kyle take me outside, but I also didn't want a scene. I'd seen the rule played out: if one of you is in trouble, you're all in trouble.

## CHAPTER 25

*Tatum*

I ran around my bedroom, grabbing anything and everything I could possibly want for Nigel's New Year's party and staying the night. Even though I was a bit anxious about meeting his friends, I was excited. It helped that Diane, Andi, and Val would be there too.

I looked in my duffel bag and ran through everything in there. Toiletries, perfume, makeup, pillow, clothes for the morning, dress, and pajamas. Damn. That didn't look right. Pajamas? What else would I take, though, a negligee? Nope. Because nothing was going happen. At least nothing like that. I would make sure of it.

As much as I really liked Nigel, maybe even to the point of falling in love with him, I would not sleep with him, nor anyone, for a long time.

"Tatum, Nigel just pulled up," my mom yelled.

I zipped up the bag and gave Gizmo a hug. "Hold down the fort while I'm gone, Gizzie." I gave him a last pat and slung my bag over my shoulder.

As I turned the corner for the living room, my mom was letting Nigel in the door. He stepped inside. "Hi,

Tate," he said with a smile.

He turned to my mom and handed her a piece of paper. "This is from my mum. It has her and Lester's phone lines listed. She said don't hesitate if you want updates."

"Thanks, Nigel. Tell your mom I appreciate it." She placed the note on the end table. "Tate, you have everything?"

"Yeah, if not, Di or Andi may have it."

Toni came running around the corner, yelling, "Bye, Nye-gul and Tatey." She had her friend Brittany with her. They both were wearing party hats they'd made. Nigel and I couldn't help but chuckle. They looked ridiculous and cute at the same time.

I picked her up. "How did you say Nigel's name?"

"Nye-gul."

Only Nigel's accent was cuter than a five-year-old's pronunciation. "That's what I thought you said. Okay, have fun tonight, Tone. Don't miss the ball drop."

"I won't." She gave my cheek a zerbert and then struggled to get down. Toni ran off with her friend, yelling, "Daddy, Tatey said I stay up for the ball drop."

"Can you get going before she thinks she's going to the party with you too?" My mom laughed.

Nigel grabbed my bag and we took off.

On the ride over to his other house, we took a similar route. Winding, narrow roads with corners you couldn't see around until your car was halfway around the curve. I hated those roads. I had to take my mind off the nail-biting drive. "Sorry Toni can't pronounce your name correctly."

Nigel laughed. "Don't be sorry, it was cute. She's a, as you guys say, a pistol."

"Yeah, she is, that's for sure. So you mentioned

dinner, are we ordering pizza?"

I glanced over at Nigel. Thankfully he didn't take his eyes off the road. "Uh no, Mom and Bren are cooking for us."

"Oh wow, that's too much. They're cooking for everyone?"

"No, silly," he laughed. "Just the four of us."

"Huh?"

"You'll see when we get there."

Nigel had a talent for not informing me of things in full before we did them. I'd have to work on that. Surprises were one thing, lack of communication were another.

He drove into a gated community with enough trees to start a nursery—and they were all enormous, mature trees. What was more impressive were the homes. They were small mansions.

"Dear Lord, Nigel . . . is your other house back here?"

"Yeah, we're almost there."

The homes were all different. Each property had the house sitting way back from the street, with acreage on all sides. I'd never seen such a rich area before.

Nigel pulled down what seemed to be the last street in the back of the community. He pulled in the drive of an enormous English Tudor mansion. An old Saab 900 and an Alfa Romeo were already parked in front of us.

Nigel helped me with my bag and led me into the garage. A 1950s Cadillac convertible was parked in there. "Oh my gosh, Nigel. Whose car is that?"

He turned back around and smiled. Pride was beaming off him. "That's my dad's 1957 Cadillac Eldorado Biarritz convertible. It's a classic."

"Yeah, no shi—"

"There you are." Mrs. Marshall flung the garage door open and stood at the top of the steps. "Dinner is almost ready. Nigel, did you give Mrs. Duncan that note?"

"Yes, Mum."

"Hi, Tatum. Come on in."

We stepped into the house, and I did everything I could not to stand there and gawk like an idiot. The house was so cool. We walked into the kitchen, which was the size of my living room and kitchen put together. The smell of food made my stomach growl.

"Nigel, show Tatum her room and give a quick tour while we finish up."

"Well, did you want me to help you first?" I asked.

She smiled but shooed us away with her hands. "No, now go. I have it."

Nigel took my hand and led me through the house. Three bedrooms were on the main floor—that included a master and two bathrooms. On the upper level were two more bedrooms and an enormous living room. There were two more bathrooms up there. All of the house was similar to the outside: Spanish fixtures married to an English Tudor.

"The house is so cool. But why would you buy this for such a small amount of furniture?" I asked.

Nigel turned to me before we went back down to the main floor. "Dad wanted a house for us in the States anyway, for when we visited Mum's family. This is the house he bought for us. After he died, Mum couldn't live here. She met Lester, and he bought the house they live in now."

I needed a notebook to keep Nigel's past straight.

"Nigel? Tatum? Dinner is ready," Mrs. Marshall called.

Nigel and I walked into the large dining room with a Spanish ornate chandelier over the dark wood table.

Bren walked in carrying plates covered with delicious-looking choices. "Hey, Tate. Happy New Year!"

"Thanks. Happy New Year to you. Can I help?"

"Nah, we have it. You sit here." Bren pointed to a chair on a corner.

They brought the side dishes to the table in nicer china than you'd see in the Smithsonian and took their seats. Nigel next to me, Bren across from us. Mrs. Marshall sat at one end of the table, and the other was left empty. The table was set as if we were in a fine-dining restaurant, with white table runners and napkins with crystal glassware and gold china. I was afraid to pick up the water goblet.

Nigel whispered, "We say a prayer."

I nodded.

Everyone lowered their heads and Mrs. Marshall spoke. "God, we thank you for this food. And Harry, I miss you. We all do. And we've welcomed Nigel's new girlfriend to the family. This is Tatum."

I wasn't sure if I should say hi, or just let her talk.

"Lester is well and sends his love too. We'll love you forever, Harry. Happy New Year."

Bren and Nigel said, "Happy New Year, Dad."

I had never spoken to Grandma out loud in front of other people, but this seemed to comfort them. It was comforting, but it made me think of my grandma being able to hear and see me. That idea confused me. Could the dead really see and hear us?

After grace, we dug in. On my plate was the broiled fish Mrs. Marshall had prepared for everyone. In serving bowls on the table she had an assortment of greens and starches. All right up my alley. With our plates full, the chatter began.

Mrs. Marshall began, "Bren, did you fill the fridge downstairs?"

"Yeah, I filled it with nothing but wine and beer."

I swallowed, hard. Drinking? I supposed Di was right.

"Brenda, that is not—"

"Mom, don't call me that. You know I hate it."

"Well, sorry. It's your name."

Nigel patted my knee under the table. A signal this was going to be a potential argument.

"Yeah, well, I can change that, so don't push me. And yes, there's soda, milk and juice boxes for Nigel's friends. The real drinks are chilling for me and my friends."

"Oi, no worries. I made sure the camcorders are in place too for when Brenda's drunk off her arse, so I can blackmail her in the future." Nigel looked at his sister with raised eyebrows. I supposed that was his payback.

Bren dropped her fork and pointed. "Now listen, you shit, you and your girlfriend are under my watch tonight, so don't make it difficult for you when Mum leaves."

Nigel laughed. But I didn't know what she meant by that and wasn't sure I wanted to.

Mrs. Marshall huffed but kept nibbling at her food. "Nigel, you have the snacks ready?"

"Yes, Mum. The rest are in the cupboard."

His accent was so cute.

Mrs. Marshall put her fork down and lifted her glass of wine. "So, Tatum. Nige says you're a junior. Any college plans yet?"

The thought of college brought a pain to me,

remembering my talk with my parents about my options in life just before I broke up with Zach. "Not really. I just found out my grandmother left me some money for college tuition. I hope to get some kind of scholarship, though, to help."

"Oh, that would be nice," Mrs. Marshall said. "Nigel got a full ride to Mizzou."

"You did? That's great."

He looked at me, clearly not wanting to talk about himself, because he lowered his head. "Yeah, it's no big deal."

"What? Yes, it is, Nigel." Mrs. Marshall said. "It's a very big deal."

"Getting a free ride to an Ivy league school . . . now that's a big deal. Not a state school."

"Nigel, you can be such a snob sometimes," Bren said. "A free ride is a free ride. You don't even want to know how much Jake's student loans are because he didn't get any help from scholarships or his family. Don't be such a snobby dickhead."

Mrs. Marshall finished off her wine. "Let's not talk like that at the table, Brenda. Do you know what you're interested in, Tatum?"

I suppose no family is perfect. And maybe there was nothing wrong with talking like that to each other. In my family, my mother would have hauled off and smacked me right off my chair if I talked like that, whether at the table or not.

"Physical therapy? Maybe." They didn't want to hear what I really wanted to do.

Nigel put his fork down and turned to me. "Tate, say it."

"Say what?" Everybody was staring at me. "What do you mean, Nige?"

"You're not saying something."

Mrs. Marshall laughed. "Oh, I love how he can read people. You have such a talent, Nigel."

"Yes, our precious golden boy." Bren snickered and then threw back her glass of wine. Nigel stuck his tongue out at her and she reciprocated. It appeared to only be sibling banter.

"Just say it, Tate. There's no right or wrong answers." Nigel patted my knee.

I took a deep breath. "I want to be a coroner." I watched each of their faces.

Mrs. Marshall dropped her head, looking down at her plate. Bren raised her eyebrows, looking amused. I looked at Nigel.

He had the most content expression, completely relaxed. "I think that sounds brilliant. Utterly brilliant, Tatum."

"Not sure my mom agrees. She's pushing for physical therapy. My dad thinks it's awesome, though. He's not squeamish like my mom."

Nigel turned toward his mother. "Did I tell you Tatum's father was a boxer?"

"Not sure they want to hear more about me or my dad, Nigel."

"Why not, you're fascinating. I love hearing about you and your family."

I noticed Bren's face. She had her head tucked down, but her eyes were watching Nigel and me. She kept taking her lips and tucking them in. We made eye contact and she smiled at me and nodded. She approved. Not sure how I could tell, but I just thought she did. But there was something she was laughing about. Her mom. Her mother must have said something about me beforehand. Or it could have been my big mouth talking about morbid things during dinner. I should have kept my mouth shut.

I glanced over at Mrs. Marshall.

She looked sick. "Yes, you did mention the boxing, Nigel. Bren? More wine, dear?" She stood up.

"Hell yeah, this is getting good."

Nigel shook his head. "Whatever. You know Mum is just easily grossed out."

"I am not," she yelled from the kitchen.

No. I would have agreed with Nigel. She seemed completely grossed out, at least that's how she was acting. She wouldn't even look at me.

Nigel and Bren laughed. "Yes, you are!"

Mrs. Marshall came back with the bottle of wine and refilled her glass and Bren's. I wasn't sure how old Bren was, but maybe she was twenty-one.

I thought it was best to take the attention off of me and my morbid career choice. "Do you go to college, Bren?" I asked.

"I'm a senior at St. Louis University. I'm getting my bachelor's degree in mathematics. I'd like to be an elementary teacher."

I couldn't imagine working with kids like Toni all day. I love Toni, but teaching her math, I'd shoot myself. "Working with kids sounds like a lot of fun."

"Nigel, let's get dessert out before it gets too late. I know you guys need to get ready before your friends start showing," Mrs. Marshall said.

Nigel went to the kitchen. We could hear the fridge open and slam shut. Then a drawer jerked open, shuffling utensils around. Nigel was not the most refined in a kitchen.

Bren got up and walked in there. "Dear god, do you have to be so loud? Move."

To make the awkward moment pass, I wanted to use the time wisely. "Thank you for having me for dinner, Mrs. Marshall. I appreciate it. This was very nice."

"Oh, you are so welcome, dear. We do this every New Year's Eve. You're the second girl Nigel has invited. Last year was his last girlfriend. Hopefully you'll be back next year."

Oh my . . . Why did she say that to me? She didn't think Nigel would still be with me come next New Year's. I'd seen this kind of behavior before. Moms and their sons. Some moms can't handle their son's giving so much attention to another female, and they get jealous. They fear the girlfriend will take them away from them forever. Never would I understand that behavior.

Bren and Nigel walked back in the dining room and Mrs. Marshall sat up, adjusting her ass in the seat, again, not looking at me. What was this woman's deal? I thought she liked me.

Bren set the carrot cake down in front of her mother. "Here. Jake will be here soon."

"How come he didn't join us this year for dinner?" Mrs. Marshall asked.

"He had plans with his family. They were going to dinner," Bren said.

Mrs. Marshall sliced the cake. "Would you like a piece of cake, Tatum? It's carrot."

Nigel grinned. He must have told his mom that was a flavor I liked. "A small piece, please. I have to fit in that dress."

After dessert, I insisted on clearing. In the kitchen, Bren whispered to me, "Just ignore Mum. She realized how serious Nigel is with you. Now you're a threat." Bren walked off.

A threat? What the hell did that mean? A threat to who? Her? Exactly what I feared. When did dinner take a nasty turn? After I mentioned being a coroner. Damn it, I should have kept my trap shut.

The kitchen was cleared and put back together along with the dining room. Mrs. Marshall had a plate covered with foil wrap in her hand and her purse over her shoulder.

"I'll be back in a few. Call if you need anything. I gotta go, Lester is waiting to eat."

She gave Nigel and Bren a peck on their cheeks and walked out through the garage. The moment the garage door closed and we heard her Alfa Romeo drive off, Nigel and Bren gave each other a high five.

"Let's party!"

Nigel took my hand and pulled me toward the bedrooms down the hall from the kitchen. "We're getting dressed in the master."

"As long as I don't hear anything, it didn't happen," Bren yelled back.

## CHAPTER 26

*Tatum*

Nigel shut the master bedroom door behind us. "Tatum, you can take the bathroom. I'll stay out here."

"What did Bren mean by that?"

He laughed, grabbing my duffel bag for me and handing it over. "Just being a shit. Ignore her. She thinks we'll have sex. That's what."

"In your father's home? She doesn't know me very well." His father wasn't the only reason why.

"That's Bren. Trust me, she's an ass, but cool. Did you see the way she looked at you? She likes you, Tate."

"Yeah, probably because your mom doesn't." I took my bag and turned for the bathroom.

Nigel put his hand on my shoulder. "Hey, that's not true. She likes you or she wouldn't have invited you for dinner."

"Her dislike came during dinner. I shouldn't have said anything about becoming a coroner at the table. It's gross."

"Hey." Nigel wrapped his arms around my waist.

"Don't do that. Just because Mum's a wuss doesn't mean she doesn't like you. Stop talking rubbish."

One of the ways you could tell Nigel was getting worked up was by his accent. It became clear and strong.

"Okay, fine. She likes me." I wasn't about to bring up what she'd said to me about Nigel bringing a different girlfriend last year. Maybe Mrs. Marshall "liked" her too, at first.

Nigel gave me a quick peck and backed away. "Go get dressed. We don't have much time." He looked at his watch. "People should begin arriving in half an hour."

The bathroom was big enough for three girls to get ready. It had a double-wide vanity with a Jacuzzi tub separate from the shower. The bathroom was bigger than my bedroom. With my makeup done, hair curled, and the dress that Nigel had bought me on, as well as my shoes and a little perfume, I was ready. I stepped out into the bedroom and it was empty. But someone had dimmed the lights and lit candles, and jazz played softly in the room. Completely romantic. I glanced around to see where the music was coming from and there were small speakers in the walls. They were camouflaged, matching the paint color.

Voices came from inside the house. Not just Nigel and his sisters, but a lot of other voices I didn't recognize.

Someone knocked on the bedroom door. "Tate, you in there?" It was Val.

"Come in."

Val walked in the bedroom and shut the door behind her. She looked around and then at me with a smile. "Oh my gosh . . . has Nigel seen you yet?"

"No, I just got done in the bathroom. Hey, I love your dress."

She shrugged. "Thanks, Mom got it from Famous. This room . . . " she raised her eyebrows in a sultry way. "Nigel is so romantic, huh?"

I gave Val a hug. "I know, but nothing is happening. Especially tonight."

"Uh huh, yeah right, sure." Val chuckled.

"I swear nothing will happen in here, or anywhere, for that matter. Not tonight. So, when did you get here? I'm scared to walk out, I don't know anyone."

"Jeez. You are nervous. I just got here, but it seems like there's just a few people here for now. Ohh . . . and Jake is here."

"Who's Jake? I heard his name a lot during dinner."

"Bren's boyfriend. He's hot. Haven't you met him yet?"

"No, but I will. It's good to see you, Val."

She stepped up to me and took my hands. "I'm sorry Scotty and I did that to you and Nigel a month ago. You know I would never want to hurt you. We've been friends for too long."

"I know, but thanks for saying that. Nigel and I needed to do this on own our terms."

She dropped my hands and lightly elbowed me. "And you two cats did. He's pretty great, isn't he?"

The thought of Nigel made that different breed of butterfly flutter in my stomach again. My hands became moist. "He is. He's great."

"What is that I see?" She backed up, eyes expanding. "Oh my god . . . you're totally falling for him. I knew it. I knew you two would be perfect for each other. I knew it."

The door flew open. Nigel stepped inside. "You

knew what? How beautiful m'lady is?"

I had to swipe my hands on the sides of my dress, and the damn sequins scratched me.

"Uh huh . . . I'll be out here when you decide to make an appearance, Tate." Val walked out and shut the door behind her.

Nigel scanned every inch of me from head to toe. "Oi, I'm one lucky guy . . . you look great in that dress." He pulled me into an embrace. "Can you come out so I can introduce you to some other friends?"

"Of course." I didn't hesitate, I kissed his perfect lips.

"We better walk out there before it's too late."

Nigel held my hand and took me around the house, introducing me to everyone. The two of us went from room to room, and more people kept arriving, but not Andi and Di. Music followed us in all of the major rooms. Nigel checked the closet in the hall that housed the equipment. I had never seen such audio equipment before, but they had it. Nigel made sure Bowie, the Replacements, the Smithereens, and many others had us entertained for eternity. An hour later, I'd met everyone. Nigel had around eight friends there, Bren four. And Val was right, Jake was a total hotty.

After Nigel and I made our rounds, we went into the kitchen for a drink. Di and Andi walked in. I threw my arms up and gave them a greeting hug. I had been getting worried they wouldn't show. I was excited to see Andi wearing her new strapless, sequined dress. Di wore a pink thin silk dress with a flirty look. The back of her dress swooped down to the middle of her back. It reminded me of club attire from the 1930s.

"Damn, Di. Hope you don't get cold tonight." I laughed.

That caught Nigel's attention, and he glanced over at her.

"I told you," Andi said, rolling her eyes.

"If you don't like it, Andi, I told you to look the other way." Di cocked an eyebrow at me. "She thinks it's somewhat see-through."

I stood there laughing at them acting like an old married couple, bickering with each other.

"Tate, your drink?" Nigel asked.

I didn't know what to say. Alcohol had never touched my lips before. But I wasn't one to drink much soda and I wasn't about to ask for a juice box, even though that was my preferred drink. Assuming Bren meant it when she said they had them. "Uh, Andi, what are you having?"

Andi looked like she couldn't believe her ears. I supposed I shouldn't have put her on the spot like that. I chuckled. "Di, what are you having?"

"Tate and I will have a glass of red wine, Nigel. Thank you." Di was cool and confident in her response.

He looked at me. I nodded, giving the approval.

Nigel's friends who we'd met at the mall walked into the kitchen. Nigel popped up. "Tate, you remember my mates, Tommy and Jessie?"

"Of course." I waved. "Thanks again, guys, for earlier."

The curly blond, Tommy, looked at Di. "You're welcome, Tate. Hi, Di."

Di gave him a thorough scan. "Hi, Tommy. Glad to see you again." Her voice was smoother than her silk dress. Now I understood why she wore the silky number.

Jessie stepped up to Andi. "What are you drinking? Your hands are empty."

I could see her swallow. "Oh, how about whatever you're having. Thanks."

"You got it." Jessie went in the kitchen with Nigel and grabbed the Jack Daniels bottle.

Andi jerked her head toward me, and mouthed, "I can't drink that!"

Nigel handed me and Di our glasses of wine. After Di thanked Nigel, she and Tommy walked off to another room together.

Andi stepped up to me and grabbed my arm, and whispered in my ear, "Dear god, Tatum . . . it will kill me. That shit is going to be strong."

I held her hand, trying to loosen her grip. "Hey, Jessie. Can you put a lot of Coke in it?"

"Of course. Did you think I was pouring straight Jack?"

Andi walked over to the counter. "Oh, no . . . she's just a worry wart. You're fine."

Nigel snickered, witnessing the exchange, and led me away to the living room, heading straight for the fireplace. We sat on the stone hearth. Warming my bare back felt nice. I loved listening to the crackle of wood burning.

Nigel sipped his beer. I couldn't believe how right Di was—everyone was drinking. And beer was probably the weakest drink there.

"Why didn't you tell me you've never drunk before?" Nigel asked.

"How could you tell?"

"Tatum, give me some credit. I have eyes." He patted my knee.

"It shouldn't be . . . but I suppose it's embarrassing. Seeing everyone being so nonchalant about it. I don't know."

"Never be embarrassed. About anything, especially with me." He leaned over and kissed my lips. He backed up, just a bit. Our noses almost touched. "You look beautiful tonight. Happy anniversary."

"Thanks. Happy anniversary to you too. And I love the dress." I ran my hand down his leg. "As usual, you look good in the jeans and boots." Nigel wore a white button-down shirt, sleeves cuffed. His signature look. So frickin' sexy.

He took a drink of his beer and looked away. I dropped my hand.

"What do you think of this house?"

I glanced around at the beautiful living room, which was the width of the whole house. In the middle of the room, the floor dropped down two steps, like I'd seen in old James Bond flicks. On the other side of the living room was a baby grand piano. A lone picture of Nigel and his family sat on it. "I love it. It's very pretty."

"Brilliant. Because when I graduate college, it's mine."

I almost dropped my glass. "What? This house is yours? I thought it was your dad's?"

"Mum is signing it over to me the day I graduate from college. Bren is getting money."

I took a drink of the wine, ignoring how dry it was. "Holy Toledo. That's awesome."

He was inheriting a house? A mansion, or at least to me it was a mansion. I would be lucky to get a little bit of money for graduating from college. And Nigel was getting a house like this? He was very lucky. But on the flip side, he'd lost his dad. I wouldn't prefer a house over having my dad around.

I finished my first glass of wine and felt all of the anxiety disappear. Now I didn't care who I had to meet.

That scared me. No more alcohol. I didn't like the feeling that someone else controlled me, and at the moment the someone else was the alcohol.

Moments later Nigel came back with a fresh cold beer. "So why don't you tell me 'bout the bully at the mall today. How do you know him again?"

"Streakin' in the park time," Scotty yelled as he came running in the room.

Bren jumped up from the built-in seats in the floor. "Hot Damn shots! Let's go, Tatum. You first."

"Me?" I looked at Nigel.

He tossed his beer back. "Go get 'em, Tate."

He was no help at all. I didn't want to look like a rookie in front of everyone. "Val, Di, and Andi, I need you."

We girls gathered in the kitchen, around the counter. Nigel gave me a kiss for good luck, but laughed as he walked off. I reconsidered kissing him any more for the night.

Bren had her girlfriend, Anna, there. Anna seemed cool. She had a slight Indian accent. Anna pulled me in between her and Bren. "Now, don't sip it like a girl, Tatum. You throw the shit back. If you don't, it'll burn a hole right through your throat."

Everyone in the kitchen laughed.

*Holy crap, what am I doing?* "Look, Anna, I can't. I'm not sure what this is."

Bren chuckled. "You'll soon find out, and then you'll never forget!"

*Come on, Tatum. Put your big-girl pants on. Everyone is watching you. You can do this if everyone else is.* I looked over at Andi. She was breaking a sweat, brushing her hair out of her eyes. Di stood there, ready to jump into the action. Val had a ridiculous grin on her face. Shit, she looked as if she'd had too much already.

Bren filled six shot glasses with red-colored liquid. I could smell the cinnamon. It was strong. "What is this again?"

I was scared to death. The smell alone warned me to run in the other direction.

"It's called 'Hot Damn,' Tatum. You like cinnamon-flavored candy, right?"

"Eh, it's okay." I loved cinnamon, but this wasn't candy.

Anna handed the rest of the shot glasses out to the girls. Bren handed me mine. "On the count of three, we throw it back, girls. No whining or moaning. We're women, this is nothing."

She glanced at me. "Ready, Tate?"

I nodded. Then I noticed Nigel and his friends were standing on the other side of the kitchen, watching us. Nigel nodded at me, raising his beer can. Great, he was watching the whole damn thing.

Big-girl panties on, I took a deep breath. Andi kept taking deeper breaths, so loud you could hear her. I supposed I wasn't the only nervous one.

"One. Two. Three," Bren said.

Everyone but for me and Andi threw them back. Andi and I stared at each other. *Together, Andi.* She gave me a nod. *Go!* We closed our eyes and I threw mine back. The Hot Damn burned through the lining of my esophagus, then down my chest. I would soon die. I swallowed it all. It couldn't be helped. I shot fire out of my mouth. "Damn. That shit burns." I closed my eyes and shook my head. That didn't help. Hot Damn was some nasty shit.

"Again," Bren yelled.

I popped my eyes open because I couldn't believe my ears. Bren was refilling the six shot glasses. "Thanks, but I'm done, Bren."

She filled mine. "No, you're not, we go again. It's tradition."

"What the hell kind of tradition is this?" I asked. Damn. I wasn't sure if my words were slurred. I glanced over at Nigel for the answer. Jessie was whispering in his ear. And my boyfriend had a scheming grin on his face. Shit. That was my answer.

"One. Two. Three," Bren said.

Everyone threw them back. Andi and I did on our own count. And we both shot fire out of our mouths afterward. I placed my hands on the edge of the counter and bent over, taking deep breaths. I needed to since I'd burned my airway.

A hand patted my back. "One more and we're streakin'," Bren said.

*Oh god, I'm not ever going home. This is going to kill me. What did I do to deserve this?* My inner voice cried. I stood up, hanging on to the counter, feeling oozy. "Bren, I'm done."

"Third time's a charm. Come on, little Tatey."

"Please don't call me that."

Third time was a charm? It dawned on me . . . Nigel was my third boyfriend. Maybe he was a good-luck charm.

Bren poured another round, and I noticed Andi was hanging on to the edge of the counter too. One more and we wouldn't be able to walk. I had to look at everyone. I could still see their faces, though. That was good news. Maybe I wasn't as bad off as I thought. But by the looks of it, they were all Hot Damn shot pros. *Where have I been my whole life? In a fricking closet.*

One more on our own count, and Andi and I blew so much fire out of our mouths, we ran for a cup of ice water. We stood facing each other in the kitchen, chugging.

We finished it off, and my throat felt better. Not back to normal, but better. "We survived, Andi! We did it."

She took a deep breath. "I had Jack on top of it. Tate, my night will be over soon if we don't stop drinking. I have to watch the ball drop."

Bren yelled, "Everyone outside in five minutes."

Andi grabbed my arm. "Dear god, Tatum. I can't get undressed. Matt would kill me."

"Does that mean if it weren't for Matt, you wouldn't care?"

"I would care. Just not like I do now."

This is where it got tricky. I would love to have said, *Don't worry about it. He's not here and I won't tell. Do what you want.* I couldn't be that devious. But then again . . . maybe just a little deviousness couldn't hurt. "Do what you want, Andi. If you do go through with it, I won't say a word. Your call." I patted her shoulder and walked off to find Nigel.

He was in the hall. "Can I talk to you, Nige?"

He excused himself from another high school friend he was talking to and we stepped in the bedroom and closed the door. "We're not doing this, are we?"

"Not unless you really want to. But I wasn't planning on it."

I flopped on the bed. "Oh, thank god."

He crawled in next to me. "I take that as a no."

"You take right."

Nigel glanced at the clock. "It's almost ten. Mum should be stopping by soon."

I flung myself up, getting a bad head rush. "Ouch." I held my head. "I don't want her to see me like this."

"You're not drunk, are you?"

"No, just got up too fast. But if I had another drink, I probably would be."

"Let's get you something to snack on and ibuprofen before a headache starts."

Nigel doctored me up. "Tate, do you want to slip out of the dress?"

Now I knew I was drunk. It sounded like Nigel had propositioned me. "Excuse me?"

"Not that, silly. I mean, it's cold. You may want to put pants and a sweater on. We can just go out there and watch the others. Trust me, this streakin' will not end well. Someone always does something stupid."

"How often do you guys do this?"

"Just parties. Not much at all. Maybe twice a year. But for sure on New Year's Eve."

"Yeah, let me change real quick. I wouldn't want anything to happen to the dress."

Nigel walked over to the closet and grabbed a large comforter off the top shelf. "We can take this for us to sit on."

"Oh thanks, that looks perfect." I grabbed my dress hanger and reached back for the zipper.

I felt Nigel's hands on mine. "Here. Let me unzip you."

It was a short zipper, since the dress was cut so low, but Nigel made sure to drag it out, letting his fingers slowly glide down my backside. His hands were warm and soft, exactly what I wanted to feel on my body. That's all it took for Nigel to undo me.

The dress fell to the floor, and I turned around. I stood there in black lace panties and rose-colored petals over my nipples. Otherwise, completely naked. Nigel took a deep breath, not sure where to look. His stare, mostly, stayed on my breasts.

"Oh my god. Tatum? I ah. We should. Uh." Nigel took a deep breath.

I wasn't nervous that Nigel was seeing me almost naked. I felt good. I reached up to his chest and played with his top button. "Nigel, I wanted you to see me."

He took another breath. "Oi, Tatum. I uh. I see. Oh god do . . . I see, m'lady."

His accent took me there. I rested my hand on his shoulder. "Kiss me, Nigel, before you hurt my feelings."

I didn't need to say it twice. Nigel took hold of my body and kissed my lips with such ferocity we could have caught fire from the friction. Within seconds of being on a radical roller coaster kiss, someone banged on our bedroom door.

"Stop it in there, let's go. Now," Bren yelled.

I backed away from Nigel and pulled the covers off the bed and up to my chest.

"Damn it, Bren. We'll be right there. Don't you come in here." Nigel walked over to the door and locked it.

"Then you better have your arses outside in two."

Nigel thudded his fist on the door. "Arse wipe, go."

You could hear her laughing, and then the laughter fading.

Nigel walked over and gave me the predator stare—lowered eyelids, but only focused on me. He appeared to be still hot from our kiss. I had to get far away from the bed. Making out was one thing, but being next to a bed, unclothed, was another invitation.

"Blimey, she's an arse."

I grabbed my clothes from the duffel and slipped a sweater over my head. "It's okay. To be honest . . . it would have led to something I wouldn't feel comfortable with right now anyway. Besides, those stupid Hot Damn shots have me in a fog."

Nigel came behind me, sliding his hands on my hips. "I would never force you, Tate."

"I know."

Nigel waited for me at the door with the comforter in his hands.

## CHAPTER 27

*Tatum*

Nigel and I walked through a quiet, empty house. He escorted me out into the backyard through the glass sliding doors. Their property was big, and in the very far back was a wall of enormous evergreen trees and bushes. It made a great privacy wall. We walked through the bushes and trees, and just beyond that there was a dark park.

"Oh wow, what park is this?"

"Lincoln Valley. It's really private. Nothing around but the few houses here that back up to it."

"I guess this is the perfect place then, huh?"

"Exactly." Nigel took my hand. "Be careful. The ground is crap here."

He escorted me a way out into the park. Only the neighboring properties supplied any light for us.

We came up on the others, all standing in a line.

"About time you two decided to join us. Now, everybody strip down to your skivvies."

"Not this time, Bren. Tate and I are sitting this one out."

"Okay, no time to argue. Mum will be back in a

while." Bren looked at everyone else in the line. "The rules are, run down to the road. Come back up, and the first person back here at Lame-arse and Tate wins. No cheating. Run all the way down to the road."

Everyone shed their clothes, but for their underwear—the girls got to keep their bras on too. Nigel shook the comforter out and laid it on the ground, off to the side. I was glad the snow had melted.

"Nigel, give us a count," Bren said.

I didn't want to look at all the different asses. They could have been posing for an underwear ad. All sorts of colors and styles. I hid my laughter. It was best to stare at my girlfriends' asses. Andi, Val, and Di were really cold. Poor Di didn't even have a real bra on, she had a silk, short, slip-type cami.

Nigel stood next to our blanket. "Ready. Set. Get your arses down that hill."

Everyone took off. Andi immediately tripped, landing face-first. I gasped, reaching out for her, as if that would help.

Di grabbed her and pulled. "Dear lord, Andi. We're not even five feet. Come on."

Jessie and Tommy ran back toward them and took Andi's hands—of course trying to see as much of her as possible. Out of all the girls there, Andi was still shaped the biggest. Not a surprise, considering Andi would give Dolly a run for her money.

They took off down the hill. Once they all made it over the crest, we couldn't see them anymore. But we could hear plenty of giggling and cussing. Bren was the loudest of all.

Nigel took a seat next to me and wrapped us in the blanket. "You warm enough?"

"Oh yeah, I have clothes on, you to cuddle, and this

blanket. I'm good."

He kissed the side of my head. "Brilliant."

"How long will they be gone?"

"At least ten minutes. The trick is finding the road in the dark. Or any road, for that matter." He laughed.

"Oh dear . . ." I chuckled.

"That gives us some time. So, tell me who that was at the mall today. That was more than just some jerk from school."

The night was going perfectly. The last thing I wanted to talk about was Asshole Star Football Player—or Zach. But after tonight, I felt so close to Nigel. I trusted him even more. Being in a relationship with him was the one thing I was happy about and looked forward to. This would have to come out sooner or later. The truth hurt, but I had to remember I wasn't alone.

"Kyle was my boyfriend a while back."

"You dated that asshole?"

"That asshole wasn't one at first. He was nice, and fun. Believe it or not."

"Not." Nigel laughed. "Go on, what happened?"

Nigel didn't seem jealous or upset, which was great. I could breathe. "As time went on, his true colors showed. Plain and simple. I found out the hard way he has a temper. He'd fly off the handle over the silliest things. Like going to the mall without him. If I wanted to stay home for the night. Anything. Everything. You name it."

"So you broke up?"

"Yeah. Something like that."

"How long did you date him?"

"Jeez, I suppose it was about seven months or so. Not too long."

"That's a long time, Tate. My first girlfriend, we dated for two months. Okay, so tell me about this other guy, Zach?"

Moving onto another subject was fine with me. Even if it was the one that hurt me more. "Oh, Zach is still off-limits. But we dated seriously for a month."

"Why is he still off-limits? Do you still love him?" Nigel's voice dropped.

I thought about that. Did I? I cared about Zach, a lot. I loved him. But was I still in love with him? The thought made me think of Nigel and my feelings for him. There was no way I'd walk away from Nigel. But I hadn't thought I could survive without Zach, and here I was. Could I survive without Nigel? I could survive without any guy. But would I want to? No. I would not want to live without Nigel, either.

"I love Zach. I'm just not in love with him anymore. But I think I'll always be somewhat protective of him."

"Protective? Why?"

"Zach isn't allowed to make a lot of his own decisions in life. He has a different kind of family than we do. Let's leave it at that." Nigel's handsome face was waiting for an answer he could live with. "Someone else has my heart now, anyway."

Nigel pulled me closer, moving me on top of him. "Good. Because someone else has my heart too—you."

"Tell me about your past girlfriends, Nige."

"I had a few. Amanda was my first, for two months. Then Stephanie, we dated for a month. Then Janie, we dated the longest—nine months."

"What happened?"

"I guess I discovered her true colors too. She was bossy and demanding. And I heard she was telling private stuff about me to her girlfriends. I didn't appreciate the . . uh . . . we'll call it, attention. She made it harder and harder for me at school."

"I'm intrigued. Share?"

"Just stuff. Private."

"I'm your girlfriend. Now is it private?"

Nigel gave me a kiss. "She was a bit too open about our intimate relationship."

I immediately wanted off of Nigel's lap. "Did you two?"

Nigel nodded. "Did you sleep with Kyle?"

Did I sleep with Kyle? It was nothing like that. I sat next to Nigel and looked out into the dark park, not hearing or seeing anyone or anything, but for a slight breeze, barely moving the leaves. We were alone.

"Tatum, please?"

"It wasn't my choice."

Nigel grabbed my arm. "What? What are you saying, Tatum?"

It became warm outside, like someone turned on the furnace. "I didn't want to with Kyle."

"He raped you?"

"I want to change the subject. Shouldn't we hear them soon?"

"Tate, you can't be serious? Please tell me."

I looked at Nigel and took a deep breath. His face was filled with worry. Eyes and mouth concerned, silently begging me. "It wasn't consensual." I couldn't say the "R" word.

Nigel flopped back, his hands flying to his face. "Oh my god. Oh my god. I don't believe this." He flung upright. "What did the authorities say? Surely he got juvenile probation? Minimum. Something?"

"You don't know my mother. If I spoke up, she would have sent me away to an all-girls school. A prison, really. Besides, who would they believe? The star football player at school? Or just some female student who wears short skirts? Not that it's right to judge, but it's just society. And not to mention, I can't deny I was his girlfriend. Well, I had been up to the night before." I became panicked to defend myself and my actions—why I hadn't spoken up. My chest was pumping fast and my breath was heavy.

He stared at me. "Tatum, they can do tests now. It's easier to prove rape. Don't you know?" I could see half of his face even though the moon was hiding behind the clouds. He looked pitiful.

"Nigel. Stop. Please. Do not ruin my night. I'm already upset mentioning it. I want to forget about it."

He wrapped his arms around me. "Oh, m'lady. I'm so sorry." He held me tight, giving the side of my face periodic kisses.

We didn't say another word to each other for what felt like forever. We stayed in each other's arms—warm and cuddly. Safe.

Then we heard footsteps in the grass. We popped up and looked out.

"Hey, let me in so I can warm up." Jessie came up first.

Nigel opened his side of the blanket and scooted toward me. "Here, Tate." Nigel pulled me back on his lap.

Jessie got in the covers with us. All he had on was his skivvies. I slid to Nigel's other side as much as possible. I knew they were friends, but wasn't this a bit close?

Nigel put his mouth up to my ear, and whispered, "Jessie's harmless. I've known him the longest. He won't touch you." He kissed the side of my ear.

Immediate comfort. His lips were so soft and warm up against my cold ear. Besides, it tickled, in a good way.

"I don't know why Scotty thinks he can beat me. I know this park like the back of my hand," Jessie said.

"Scotty likes to compete with us. But Val usually interferes with his macho tendencies," Nigel said.

It was interesting to hear about a different side of Scotty. I had never noticed that before. But I really didn't know Scotty all that well.

Bren, along with the rest of her friends, and some of Nigel's other schoolmates, made their way back. They all had mud up their bare legs.

Bren walked up to our blanket. "What the hell are you doing in there with them?"

"I'm cold." Jessie snickered. "Like you are. You know, Bren, you should really wear a padded bra."

"You little shit—"

Jake grabbed Bren around her waist and pulled her toward the house. "Let's go. Jessie won anyway. Bren and I are taking the basement shower. No one go down there."

Bren laughed. "Yeah. For at least five minutes."

Jake, who was a big guy, stopped and threw Bren over his shoulders like a caveman. "Oh, I'll show you five minutes. We'll be at least fifty minutes. Let's go."

Her friends followed them up to the house, laughing the whole way.

"Nigel, did Tommy and the others get lost?" I was beginning to worry.

"All right, I'll go find them." Jessie stood up and stepped away from the comforter. "Wait. I hear them."

Nigel and I followed him down the hill.

"Damn it, Val. I told you that was the wrong way. I don't know why I listen to you," Scotty said.

Seconds later, we saw Val and Scotty trucking up the hill. They too had mud splattered on them. They reached us and Scotty kept walking past us, not making eye contact.

Val couldn't hide her smile. "He's pissed. I fell in the mud and accidently took him down with me. You can't see out there and it's slick." Her teeth chattered at she talked and she held her arms tight across her chest, shivering.

Scotty had her shoulders pulled up, but he seemed too pissed to care. They walked past us, grabbing their clothes off the ground and continuing up to the house, bickering the whole way.

"Nigel? Where do you think Andi and Di are? I'm really getting worried. They don't know this park like your friends do."

Nigel took my hand and we walked farther down the hill with Jessie, who still only wore his boxer briefs. Which I didn't mind, but still.

"Something happened. You're right about that. Tommy knows the park. He should have been back. Tate, stay close to Nigel, it is slick."

Nigel held my hand. I made sure to plant my feet with each step. Not only was it slick, it was steep.

Seconds later, we heard voices. "Di? Andi? Is that you?" I called out.

Jessie took off down the hill. "I see them."

I couldn't see jack.

"We're coming, Tate. It's Andi's fault we got lost. Then we got stuck. It's a long story." Di was in sight. There was mud splattered all over her, from head to toe.

"Di, what happened?"

"Well Drunky McGee there is what happened. She took us all down when she went."

"What are you holding?" The thing she held was covered in mud. It wasn't recognizable, but for what looked like long straps.

"It's Andi's damn bra. Part of the long story."

Nigel and I glanced at each other. That had to be one hell of a story.

"But I'll tell ya, Tate . . . when she complains about backaches, I don't blame her. This thing soaked with mud alone probably weighs a good seven pounds."

"Diane?" I tried to keep a straight face. "Did Andi find a mud pool? I mean . . . how is the bra soaked in mud?"

"Yeah, all part of Drunky McGee's shenanigans story."

Tommy was in sight, but it looked as if Andi was on his back. You could hear him breathing. "Dear god, girl. If you could stop hitting me in the back of the head with those things we'd get up this hill faster. And I wouldn't get a headache."

"I'm sorry. What do you want me to do? Tuck them away? If I could I would, trust me," Andi said.

Nigel pulled my hand back, making me stop. He turned back to me with a big smile on his face. He was having a hard time not laughing. Nigel patted my butt. "Go back up."

We turned and trudged back up the hill, Tommy and Andi right behind us.

I grabbed her clothes. Tommy put Andi down. Both were covered in mud from head to toe. Andi looked as if she'd taken a mud bath and then rolled around in an evergreen. Sprigs and grass were sticking out from her bangs. You couldn't see anything of Andi and Tommy but their eyes.

Di was slipping her shirt over her head, not choosing

to mess her pants up. "Yeah, so genius thinks she sees the road, and takes off for what ends up being a large baseball field. And we all know how muddy the ground is right now. She stumbled and went headfirst into a branch on the ground. Tommy tried to help her up, but slipped when he lifted her."

Tommy was bent over, trying to catch his breath. "I fell because her boobs smacked me in the head. I lifted her, not realizing how those pups would fly. They should have their own zip code. Then she slid again, falling face-first on top of me."

Nigel and I couldn't help it, we laughed. I could see it happening, and it was completely like Andi. She was a mess.

Andi didn't bother putting any of her clothes back on. You couldn't see her body anyway for the amount of mud. "Zip code, my ass . . . they aren't that big. And you weren't complaining about *the girls* when we were running down there. Now were ya?"

Tommy stood in front of her, holding his clothes at his side. "No, I didn't. I quite enjoyed the view. Let's just hope I don't have a black eye in the morning." He stepped around her, heading toward the house.

"Oh, you're an ass. I'll give you a black eye." Andi looked at Nigel. "Your friend is an asshole, Nigel." She took off, cussing Tommy the whole way.

The moment we saw Andi's backside, we busted into laughter fits. Her back side was clean as new china. Spotless.

She stopped, but didn't turn around. "It's clean back there, isn't it?"

I held my breath—"Yes." I couldn't hold my laughter in another second.

She held her head high and stomped toward the

house.

Nigel and I couldn't stop laughing. Jessie picked up his clothes and put his jeans on. He took something out of his pocket. "Nigel, I'm staying out a bit longer. Don't wait for me."

I looked at what he was holding and it was a joint. Nope. I didn't want to be around that. I was pushing it already by having a few drinks.

"Di? Would you like to stay with me?"

Di stepped over to him. "Sure, Jess. I think I will."

"You two want the blanket then? Tate and I are going inside. Don't worry about the mud, Di. We'll throw the blanket in the wash."

"Thanks, Nigel. That's sweet." She took the blanket and wrapped it around her and Jessie.

It was none of my business, but it would be interesting to see what Tommy thought of Jessie and Di out here alone, since he'd made it clear earlier he was interested in her. Not my problem.

Nigel and I headed toward his backyard. A mobile rang. But we didn't own a phone. Nigel and I looked around our feet.

"Over there, Tate. See the light flashing? Who has a mobile?"

"I don't know." I picked it up and saw a caller ID window flashing. It read: *Matt calling*.

## CHAPTER 28

*Tatum*

I dropped the ringing phone. I didn't mean to. But for some reason, the name listed on the caller ID scared me.

Nigel reached down for the phone. "Tate, careful. These are expensive." He read the same thing I had. "Matt calling. Who's that?"

"Andi's boyfriend."

Nigel jerked his head up at me. "Boyfriend? She's not single?"

"No." Why would Nigel react that way? Did she have to be single? Not sure I understood his problem.

Nigel grabbed my hand and pulled. We hustled up to his house and he slid the back sliding doors open. "Anyone see Andi?"

Anna, who sat there freshly washed, pointed toward the hall. "I think she went in that bathroom to shower. She was covered." Anna laughed.

Nigel and I knocked on the bathroom door. "Andi, you in there?"

The phone stopped ringing. I was thankful. Every time it buzzed, it made my breathing kick up a notch, and not in a good way. The thought of confronting any of them scared me to death. I was moving on. I didn't want to be anywhere near the Bertanos.

"I am, Tate. Hold on," Andi answered.

Nigel handed me the phone and kissed my forehead. "I'll be in the kitchen getting us drinks." He walked off.

Amazing how I didn't feel buzzed anymore. Maybe seeing the caller ID sobered me.

Andi cracked open the door and pulled me inside. She locked the door behind her.

"Oh my god . . . that was amazing!"

All I could see were Andi's teeth and eyes. "So you're not mad?"

"I didn't say that. Tommy's still an ass, but it was fun."

"Good."

She glanced down to my hands. "Is that my mobile?"

I handed it to her. "How did you get this? Not saying you can't afford one, but . . . you know." The sad fact was, Andi couldn't afford a mobile. I damn well knew who could, though. I just wanted to hear her say it.

"Before they left for Italy, Matt gave it to me."

"It was ringing when Nigel and I were walking back up to the house. We found it out in the yard."

"Shit. Matt would kill me if I lost this thing. He made sure to tell me how much it cost."

"Let me step out so you can call him back."

Andi grabbed my hand. "No, stay in here and talk to me for a minute."

The hall bathroom had a Spanish feel. Like the living room with the sunken floor, the bathtub was designed like an Egyptian bath house—where you stepped down into the tub. The walls around the tub and the floor were decorated in mosaic Spanish blue and white tiles. It was something I'd never seen except in the movies. I could soak in that tub all night. Andi had the water running with bubbles rising. I could smell the lavender and oatmeal.

I sat on the toilet seat. Andi slipped off her muddy panties and stepped down into the tub. She closed her eyes as she let her body slide below the bubbles. "Oh, momma, this is nice and warm."

"Well, at least you'll smell better."

Andi rolled her eyes at me. "Oh, whatever." She rested her head back on the ledge. "Isn't this house great? I love it."

"Yeah, I like it too. You know what Nigel told me about it?"

She popped her eyes open. "What?"

Andi loved gossip.

"When he graduates college, his mom is signing it over to him."

"You're shitting me?"

"No. I shit you not."

"Tatum, are you falling in love with him? I see how you look at him, and it's different than before. And the way you talk about him. I think he's falling in love with you too."

"Really? You honestly think so?"

"Yeah. He's really protective of you. Like Zach was."

"Do me a favor and don't compare them. Because I would hope to god Nigel wouldn't up and leave me like Zach did."

"You're right. I'm sorry."

"It's okay. And I think I could be falling in love with him. I just don't want to be hurt again anytime soon.

Not saying Nigel would just up and move out of the country. But . . . you know. I thought I knew Zach, too, and well . . . I just need to get to know Nigel more."

Andi rested her forearms on the ledge, looking up at me. "I do. I get it. And so you know, I think Nigel is a great guy. You two seem good together. And he has the kind of family you can live with."

How did Andi see what was inside my mind? Maybe I should have given her more credit. "Exactly. I can live with Nigel's baggage."

"I probably shouldn't tell you this. Actually, I know I shouldn't tell you this."

Right then I knew it had to do with the Bertanos, and why I would protect them, I had no clue. "Then maybe you shouldn't, Andi."

"You know me." She rolled her eyes. "I just can't help it. Besides, it's not like it matters anyway."

Andi would always be Andi, but if she was going to stay with Matt, it would work to her benefit to keep that trap of hers shut.

"Then I'm all ears."

Andi glanced at the door, then back at me. "You know Gramps made Zach leave you?" she whispered.

"Yeah, kind of put that together from what Bobby said."

"Like I said, it doesn't matter, but from the sound of it, Gramps is making Zach live there. I don't think he's coming back, Tate. Ever."

"Andi, I kind of knew this. Anything else?" Now I was hungry for real information.

"The other girl's name is Mariacella. From what Matt says, she sounds like a tyrant."

Andi had no clue she stabbed me. She didn't mean to, and I was surprised hearing about this girl made me so jealous. That tramp had my first love, though. But Zach wasn't my last. Knowing this girl's name made her even more real. If I knew what she looked like, her face would haunt my dreams. "I'm happy for her and Zach. I wish them the best."

I stood up, needing to escape. I didn't care to hear anything more about the guy who'd ripped my heart out. "I gotta go."

"Yeah, I need to call Matt back and get out. It's almost midnight."

I left the bathroom and went back into the master bedroom to put my dress back on and freshen my lipstick.

I rejoined the party and noticed the garage door was closing. I stepped into the kitchen, and Nigel was pouring champagne.

"Nigel, was that your mom?"

"Hey, there you are. You put the dress back on. Yeah, Mom was doing her check. She took everyone's car keys. Her house is in one piece and no one is trashed, and that's about all she asks." He handed me the glass of champagne. "Here, for our toast. It's almost midnight."

The glass looked beautiful with the bubbles running up the flute.

Nigel grabbed his own glass and the bottle. "Let's go back to the living room."

We resumed our spot on their stone hearth bench.

A freshly showered Jake and Bren were messing with the logs, getting them burning nice and hot. The smell of a wood-burning fireplace said, *snuggle up and relax.*

Nigel and I were cozy at the fireplace when Jessie and Di ran in from the back. "Hey, we're taking a quick shower before the ball drops. Be back in five," Jessie said. He grabbed Di's hand and they ran upstairs together.

"I guess they're hitting it off."

Nigel glanced around the room. Bren and Jake caught his stare, and they shook their heads. Nigel patted my leg. "When Tommy hears, World War Three will break out."

"So, Tommy does like Di?"

"Yeah. But so does Jessie." He looked at me. "While you were in the bathroom with Andi, I told Tommy that Andi is off-limits, she's not single."

That's why Nigel seemed bothered by Andi's non-single status. "I only have so many single girlfriends. But I can try to find more."

Nigel grabbed me around my shoulders and squeezed. "What you waiting for? Get right on it."

The way he smiled at me warmed me more than the logs burning behind my back.

Nigel had this way of making me feel alone with him, like we were the only two people in the room. I kept examining his face, and he did the same to me. What could he have been thinking? His lips told me he wanted to kiss me, but what was he waiting for? Not sure what made me do it, but I smiled a little softer than usual. Nigel's eyes began to close as he moved forward. He got my signal to go ahead and kiss me. I met him halfway. When our lips touched, it was nothing short of warm and tantalizing energy running from my head down to my toes. I wanted to get rid of the champagne glass to allow my arms the freedom to hug him, to pull him closer, although we couldn't get any closer unless we lay on top of each other.

"It's time," Bren shouted.

I almost bit Nigel by accident.

He jerked back. "Damn it, Bren."

"Wait, sock it to Tate in a minute . . . sixty seconds, people."

Everyone came running into the living room. The music paused. Bren stood in the middle of the dropped living room floor, holding a remote in her hand, pushing buttons. Then a large TV in the corner turned on and Dick Clark's face appeared. He had a black wool coat on with a cream scarf wrapped around his neck. It looked cold in New York.

Nigel stood up and requested me to join him. He then took my champagne glass and put both of ours down on the mantel. He slid his hands onto my hips. "Happy New Year, Tate."

"Happy New Year, Nige."

Nigel looked over at the TV. Everyone was shouting, "Ten. Nine. Eight . . . Three. Two. One. Happy New Year!"

Nigel picked up our kiss where we'd left off. This time we could get closer, so I grabbed around his neck and pulled him to me. Nigel placed his hand behind my head and held me. There was nothing else in the world that could relax me more than Nigel in that moment. My body reacted to him and how he made me feel. I wasn't sure what to do.

Nigel relaxed. "Happy New Year. We have to stop," he whispered in my ear, and then kissed the side of my head. He reached for our glasses and with his free hand took mine. "I look forward to nineteen ninety with you, Tatum."

"Me too, with you."

We took a sip.

Bren came over and hugged me. "Happy New Year,

sis!"

"Sis?" I looked at Nigel, and he shrugged.

"Yeah, since you two look pretty cozy over here, I think it's getting pretty serious. Anyway, I've always wanted a sister. But Mum gave me this thing," Bren thumped her hand on Nigel's chest.

"Well, I always wanted a brother, and Mum gave me exactly that." He snickered.

"Tatum, could you take Nigel's champagne for him? I'm going to kick his arse now."

I swiftly took the glass and Nigel threw his hands up, blocking Bren's wrath. She shoved him down to the floor, and Nigel only defended himself. Bren could have bloodied something with the effort she was making, but it was a weak effort. In seconds, they turned the living room into a wrestling ring.

Val and Andi walked up to me, each holding a glass of champagne.

"Happy New Year, Tate." Val hugged me.

We exchanged wishes and stood there watching Bren roll around on the floor with Nigel. Cussing him out. "I'll show you a boy . . . I'll make sure you're too sore to even move tonight. At least I'm not a pretty boy like you are."

Nigel laughed while blocking another shove. "You're right . . . you're not pretty."

Jake, along with Bren's friends, were exchanging money, betting on who would end up with the most bruises.

"Did you see Jessie and Di? Looks like they were getting cozy. Glad someone is," Andi said. She took a sip of her champagne. "Now, this stuff isn't bad."

I would have to agree with her on both accounts. "I did see them. But have you seen anything with Jessie and Tommy?"

Val stood there trying to catch up.

"No. What now? I don't need to hear anything else bad tonight," Andi said.

"Evidently, Tommy likes Di too. And Nigel made a point of telling Tommy that you have a boyfriend, just in case he got any wise ideas."

"You do?" Val asked Andi. Her speech slurred.

"Yeah. I've been dating Matt, Zach's cousin, for about a month and a half. And trust me, Tommy is not my type." Andi looked away from us.

"Zach's cousin?" Val asked.

How I wished Andi got lost down in the park. "Andi, that wasn't public knowledge."

"Damn it. Sorry. Val, don't say anything to Nigel. I don't want to cause problems between them."

"I won't, but you've got to be kidding me? Your ex, Zach, is Andi's boyfriend's cousin?"

I nodded. "Val, promise. And that goes for Scotty. 'Cause you know he won't keep his mouth shut." Glaring at Andi, I said, "Like someone else we know."

"Look, I'm sorry. I wasn't thinking. I got a lot on my mind right now."

I wanted to snatch the champagne out of Andi's hand, but what kind of Mommy patrol would I look like?

## CHAPTER 29

*Tatum*

Moments later, Jessie broke up the wrestling match between Nigel and his sister. "Come on, Bren. If you want Nigel to play, let him go."

"Want him to play? What does that mean?" I asked Val.

"The guys are in a band. Didn't you know?"

I glanced at Andi, but looked away. Things had suddenly turned awkward between us, and I wasn't sure why she was giving me bad vibes. "I'm sure Nigel just forgot to mention it."

Nigel got up from the floor and walked over to me, fixing his shirt. His hair was standing every which way, which looked hotter than it normally did. "Hey, Tate. I'll be right back, need to set up real fast."

"Nige, why didn't you tell me you guys were in a band?"

He stood there trying to calm his hair. I almost grabbed his hand to stop him.

"Oh, the three of us just mess around. Be right back."

I wasn't sure how I felt. Was this the beginning of him not telling me things? This wasn't something that needed to be a secret. I was overreacting. Not everyone was Zach.

"Let me get us a refill. You're going to love watching him, Tate. He's so good." Val ran off toward the kitchen.

"Say it now, just say it," I said to Andi.

"No matter what Nigel doesn't tell you, it will never be as serious as what Zach never told you," she said. Her eyes looked tired. But her mouth said she was upset by something.

"What the hell does that mean?"

"It means, you can't ever figure out a fucking Bertano." She turned and walked off.

Where in god's creation did that come from? Andi had seemed fine in the bathroom earlier. What was I missing? She knew something I didn't.

Within five minutes, Nigel, Jessie, and Tommy had their instruments out and they announced they were only playing acoustics. I didn't even know what instruments they played.

Val walked over with more champagne and handed it to me. "This is going to be so cool."

Watching the guys assemble was exciting. Nigel was my first musician boyfriend. "Yeah, I guess we get a private concert now." I chuckled.

The three guys sat across the room near the front door and began playing. Nigel and Tommy had acoustic guitars, and Jessie had a small bongo. They were cute. Not only did my man play the guitar, but he could sing too. The guys played a Beatles song, "While My Guitar Gently Weeps." And then "Something." The whole time Nigel sang "Something," he looked at me, never taking his gaze elsewhere. I had never been serenaded before. And I loved it. The lyrics were so romantic, speaking of how this woman affected him. What she did to him. Hearing Nigel sing to me gave me that warm, hot-chocolate-going-down feeling. It was so romantic. That crazy butterfly was back. Every word he sang, I carefully watched his lips. Even though I was enjoying the concert, I wanted to be with Nigel. Alone. I had never been turned on by a musician before. But he was damn hot.

I could feel my eyes get heavy. Nigel almost brought me to tears. Everyone was clapping and begging for another song when they finished.

Val frowned, whispering in my ear. "Where are Andi and Di? They're missing this."

She was right. They were nowhere to be seen. "Let me go check the kitchen. I'll be right back."

They weren't in the kitchen. Then I stepped out the glass sliding doors in back and they weren't outside. I couldn't find them. I headed to the hall bathroom, and they weren't in there.

As I turned around, whispered voices came from a bedroom.

"You promise you won't tell her?" It was Andi.

I took one careful step off to the side and put my ear to the small crack to listen in.

"I promise. Now will you hurry? I hear the guys playing and I'm missing it," Di said.

"Okay, so I just talked with Matt and you're not going to believe what he told me."

"Is everything okay?"

"No." Andi took a deep breath. And then sighed.

"Andi, what is it?"

I could feel my heart beating out of my chest. I felt

guilty listening into their conversation, but I knew it had something to do with Zach. Whether the dirty bastard left me or not, I cared about him.

"Tatum can't find out. She'll be so upset if she does."

Great. It had to do with me? I was nearly sweating, waiting to hear what would upset me.

"I swear, I won't say a word."

"Zach slept with Mariacella. And I don't mean just an intimate night, it sounds as if it was out there. They're saying Gramps is making wedding arrangements soon. He wants him married by next summer to this Italian girl. Matt said Zach won't talk to anyone, he's avoiding him and Bobby. Matt also said the Leads are all pissed about something, but he didn't know what. Things are happening, but the Leads and Gramps are keeping everyone else in the dark. Please don't tell Tate. I know she's falling in love with Nigel, but this would really upset her if she heard. If I was moving on with someone else and heard Matt fucked some other girl like it was nothing, I would be upset. And you know Tatum and Zach never did it, right?"

*Zach slept with another girl? No. But he's supposed to marry her, so what would it matter? He could screw her brains out as far as I cared.*

"No, I didn't. I thought they had, with how close they were."

"No, Di. Tate is still a virgin."

They didn't know the real me. They didn't need to know what Asshole Star Football Player did to me, anyway.

"Really?"

"Yeah. Just keep this quiet. No sense in ruining her night with Zach's shit. And it sounds like he's been doing nothing but drinking and screwing girls. I know Matt's upset by Zach's changes, but honestly, I'm glad he comes home tomorrow to get away from what he's dealing with right now in Italy."

"Matt's coming back tomorrow?" Di asked.

"Yeah, early afternoon. Will you take me to the airport so I can meet him?"

I stepped away from the door and made my way back to the kitchen. I needed another drink. *I can't believe Zach was with another girl so soon. And maybe many more. Not just dating, but screwing girls. How could he do that? Doesn't he care if he loves them or not? I want to love the person I'm with. And to think I considered being with him after we were together a bit longer. Oh my god, that would have been a huge mistake. Who am I kidding? I want to cut that girl's tongue out. She was all over Zach's body. But he was all over her. All over them. Oh god, I hate him. Oh, how I hate him. He made a fucking fool out of me.*

I grabbed the bottle of Bren's Hot Damn. Bottoms up. I chugged until I couldn't ignore the burning anymore. I slammed the bottle down, blowing fire out of my mouth. That shit was hot. I put it away and got a cup of water and tossed it back.

Fucking Zach, that asshole lied to me. All the times he said no matter what would happen, he would always love me. What a fucking liar. A fucking lying piece of Italian shit.

*Screw him. I hope he enjoyed whatever her name was . . . Maria bitch.*

I grabbed what was left in the bottle of champagne and dumped it into the red plastic cup. Nigel was singing. I needed to focus on what mattered in my life. A guy who was there, who never left me. A guy who was thoughtful and had a normal family. Well . . . Bren was debatable. But still, it was clear they loved and respected each other.

I stepped into the living room, and Nigel's eyes brightened the moment he saw me. He was so cute. Man, he looked like James Dean, but with black hair.

When the guys finished playing, most everyone dispersed. Bren and Jake said they were going to pop a few pizzas in the oven.

Nigel came over to me, his hands in his back pockets. If the year were 1950, I would have sworn James Dean stood before me. "What did you think, Tate?"

I grabbed him around his neck and pulled him to my lips. Nigel moaned and wrapped his arms around my waist, lifting me and swinging me around before gently placing me back down. "Shall I take that as you enjoyed it?"

"You definitely should take it that way. I just really don't understand why you didn't tell me."

"Tell ya what? The three of us jam every once in a blue moon. We haven't even 'played,' if you can call it that, since last summer. Trust me. You'd know if I was in a band."

"Oh, okay."

"Wait. Did you honestly think I was keeping this from you on purpose?"

"Kind of."

"Tatum. Tatum. Tatum. I made you a promise, and I intend to keep it."

"Promise?"

"How many of those have you had?" Nigel laughed. "Christmas Eve . . . my house . . . I promised to never keep anything from you. No secrets."

Nigel remembered. In that moment, my heart exploded. Maybe he was the one for me. Grandma always said, *Don't question God, things happen for a reason.* I reached up and hugged him. "Thank you."

"Hey, no sweat. Let's go get a bite before bed. I'm kind of tired. How 'bout you?"

"If I don't get to bed in a while, we'll have to get the toothpicks out."

Nigel kissed the side of my head and escorted me to the kitchen.

I didn't want to see Andi or Di the rest of the night. Not because I was mad at them, but because I wasn't Meryl Streep. I had never been good at hiding my feelings. Especially if I was mad or upset. And if I saw Zach anytime soon, I'd beat the shit out of him.

I was *that* kind of upset.

# CHAPTER 30

### Zach

I was running out of time. My family's flight back to St. Louis was leaving in four hours. All of the Leads, here and in the US— my parents, Gramps, Tyler, Uncle Vito, and Auntie Rose—sat in Vito's parlor. My dad got lucky by convincing Gramps to allow Piero and Sergio to have a say as well. The more the merrier, because I knew they were on my side.

I couldn't sit. I paced the floor. Gramps sat in the cozy armchair with a stogie in his mouth. "Mariacella and Davide are very pleased with the way things are moving forward. You should be proud of yourself, Zacharia, for making her happy. For treating her like the Italian princess she is."

I wanted to vomit. "Sure, Gramps. Thank you."

My mom grabbed my arm and stopped me. "Sit. You're burning a hole in Rose's rug."

I took a seat in between my parents, across from Gramps.

"That's great news, Gramps. So then with everything in place for now, I propose you let my son go back to the States to finish out this school year," my dad said.

Gramps puffed on the stogie. "Hmmm, not sure that's a good idea."

"We've thought about it, Gramps, and we think it would work out fine. It's really just six months before he's back for the whole summer. Mariacella is happy. We know her . . . she's not a girl who will remain with one guy for very long. If you want this deal to go through next summer, and keep her happy, let Zach go home for the spring. Absence makes the heart grow fonder," Mom said.

Absence from Mariacella only meant I got to keep my sanity a while longer. If Gramps didn't allow my return, I'd have to find another way to get back home to Tatum. And there he sat across from me, worrying about nothing, content to toss my life down the sewer drain. Puffing on a fat stogie. Not a care in the fucking world. I envied his power. He called the shots. Not that I wanted to run other people's lives, but if I were in control, this would not be an issue. Maybe taking over Davide's enterprise could have some benefits. Maybe his rundown vineyard could be something if we had a crew maintaining the land.

That got me thinking.

"Gramps?" Uncle Vito said. He sat on the antique couch next to Gramps's chair. "Zacharia is aware of what is expected of him. If he wants to finish school back in the US, I don't see a problem with it. Like you said, Davide and his daughter are very happy right now. I want to keep it that way."

"Gramps, shall we take a vote on it?" my dad asked. I knew he was trying not to rush, but he kept glancing at the wall clock above Gramps's head.

Gramps took the stogie out of his mouth and rolled it

in between his fingers. "Yes, a vote. Everyone in this room who agrees to let Zacharia return to the States to finish out this school term, say 'aye.'"

My breath caught in my throat. It came down to this. And like I hoped, everyone but Gramps raised their hands. I supposed that wasn't the response he'd hoped for.

"You all do?" Gramps said.

Everyone again nodded.

I was sweating. With the back of my hand, I swiped my forehead and glanced at my watch. Now down to three and a half hours before departure.

"Okay. Fine. You can return, Zacharia, under one condition."

I didn't take my eyes off of him. He was letting me go home? I stood up. "Yes, sir?"

"You take Mariacella with you."

## CHAPTER 31

*Tatum*

Nigel and I stood in the kitchen sharing a plate of oven pizza Bren and Jake had cooked.

Nigel held a slice of pizza in one hand and kept the other hand around my waist. Since he'd finished playing, he had not taken his hands off me. I considered being nervous because of what it could lead to, but not an ounce of anxiety roamed my body. I wanted him to touch me, and not stop.

Bren and Nigel were talking about her St. Louis University schedule in the following weeks. Bren looked at me. "You know, Tate. You may want to look at SLU's medical program. If you want to be a coroner, I can help get you info."

"Oh, sure, that would be great. I appreciate it. I'm hoping to get some kind of scholarship, like I said, so the money my grandma left me will hopefully cover the rest."

Andi and Di walked into the kitchen. They tried to play it cool, but I couldn't. My blood began boiling.

Jake shook his head. "Wow. A coroner? Wouldn't that bother you?"

"What? Blood?" I glanced over at the girls. Di kept her head high, stepping up to the counter next to us and grabbing some pizza. Andi was only a B actress, and wouldn't look up. "Nope. Blood . . . guts . . . doesn't bother me."

"It's more than blood and guts. You have to saw things." Jake appeared to be bothered that it didn't bother me.

Nigel and Bren chuckled.

"Sorry, but having to saw someone's chest open to take their heart out, or what's left of it, doesn't bother me one bit. If I have to break something, I could. All in the name of science, of course."

Di sipped her wine, taking glances at me. I glared at her.

"That's my cue. I'm outta here. I don't want to hear about that stuff." Andi took a slice of pizza and left the room.

Di stayed.

The moment Andi was out of earshot, I mumbled to Di, "You and I are talking."

She nodded, not giving me the slightest glance.

"Well then, it sounds like you don't mind. I'll see if I can gather any information, too. I work with the medical department part-time."

"That would be great, Jake. Thanks."

Before Nigel finished his pizza, I wanted to speak to Di alone, since we were going to bed soon.

"Di, can you come with me for a minute?"

She grabbed her glass of wine and we stepped into the master bedroom. I closed the door, and she kept her back to me.

"So, I won't make you go back on your word, but Zach's slept with this Maria bitch? Just nod for yes, or shake your head for no."

She nodded.

"He's really marrying her this summer?"

Di nodded again. Then she turned around, but kept her distance. "You need to forget about him, Tate. You and Nigel have a good thing here."

"I know we do. And trust me, Zach isn't anywhere near the level of love I have for Nigel. I've been scorned one too many times by my boyfriends. Like Bren said earlier, third time is the charm. Right?"

Di stepped up to me. "I know it still hurts. I don't blame you. But third time is the charm. I'm glad you're moving on."

"He's drinking a lot, isn't he?"

"Sounds like it. He sounds like a mess. How much did you hear?"

"Up to the point of Andi asking you to take her to the airport tomorrow afternoon. Was there more?"

"If there was, would it matter?"

"No. No, it wouldn't. I only want to know from here on out if for any reason they want to talk to me. I'll need to avoid them."

She patted my arm. "Sounds like a plan. And so you know, since you've been watching me all night . . . I like both Tommy and Jessie."

Di was always the observant one. "I figured. Nigel told me they both like you too. Sounds as if he's waiting for World War Three to start."

"Making them butt heads is not my intention."

"I know, and I'm sure Nigel does too."

"Nigel is awesome, Tate. He really is. And his sister is so cool. A fucking freak, but cool. He seems to have a nice family."

"Yeah, I think so. At least I won't have to worry

about doing anything for the Marshalls for Nigel to stay with me."

"No joke. This is just better."

"Yeah. I can use some good old-fashioned normalcy in my life."

---

The number of guests had dwindled. Bren and Anna went around the house closing things up and turning off lights. Bren and her friends cleaned the upstairs level. Nigel's friends had the main level. Jessie, Tommy, Andi, and Di took the bedroom next to our master.

Those still awake said goodnight, and we dispersed. Nigel locked our bedroom door behind us. I went over to my duffel bag. "If you don't mind, I'd like to take a quick shower. It's kind of my bedtime routine. I won't be long, promise."

"Do you want to shower or soak?"

I remembered the Jacuzzi tub. "Oh, would it be okay to take a soak? That sounds heavenly."

"Yes, of course. Let me get you started."

Nigel went into the bathroom and opened their linen closet. "Here, if you want lavender or anything like that, it's in this cupboard. My mum used to soak with all of this shit. Every time we went to the store she would have to restock. We wondered if she just dumped everything in, she'd go through it so fast."

This would be my first time ever soaking in a two-person Jacuzzi tub. "I will do my best to not use it all, but yes, I want all of that crap!"

"Okay, knock yourself out."

I grabbed my pajamas, which consisted of an oversized t-shirt and boxer shorts, and went back into the bathroom. Nigel was rinsing out the tub. "How hot?"

"Really, Nigel?"

"Yeah, how hot do you . . . oh. Sorry. Not that." He put his hands on my hips. "But that would be an interesting answer."

Nigel's hands on me made the butterfly return. He was very tempting. If he bit his lip one more time, I would be doing the biting for him. "Nigel, I need to be honest and up front with you."

"Always."

"First, stop biting your lip." He froze, which made me laugh. "Can I ask you something?"

"Of course."

I had never been so forward with a guy before. But Nigel wasn't some guy, he was my boyfriend. "Would you want to join me in the tub?"

Nigel's eyes popped wide open.

"I don't want to have sex. Not that I don't want to with you, I'm just not ready for that. But what about a bath?"

Nigel dropped his hands and took a comfortable step back. "Sure. I can probably do that. And so you know, this is a decision we both have to agree on. I'm not ready either."

"Thanks. I hope it doesn't sound childish, but I've never done this before. Hell. I've never even stayed the night with a boyfriend before."

Nigel looked like a guy admiring his new sports car. "Of course. I promise to be on my best behavior. You get in first, I'll follow."

I adjusted the water temperature and added what oils and bubbles I wanted. I was doing more than testing the waters. I was diving into the deep end, headfirst. Then with the amount of bubbles in the tub, it would be interesting to see how Nigel reacted. Would he be comfortable enough with his manhood to do this? Not sure why I found it funny to test him.

Then I heard music playing in our bedroom. A speaker clicked in the bathroom, and then sound filtered through. The house was totally wired.

Nigel came back in the bathroom. "Just some tunes for us."

"That's great, thanks. I loved this song when I was a kid. Of course I had no clue what it was about, but still."

"Yeah, Mom used to always play "Without You" by Harry Nilsson all the time. Guess it's not the best album to play for us."

"No, it has a different meaning for everyone. I like it." I pulled my hair back in a ponytail. "It's fine. I feel like I can't live without you either, Nigel."

He took a deep breath and glanced elsewhere. "Let's get in."

I was becoming more familiar with that look. He had made it twice during the party. Both times he was trying to control himself. This was the same.

We took our clothes off at the same time, facing each other. I was careful not to stumble when taking my panties off, falling over into the tub, because Nigel's physique was right off a romance novel cover. The kind I would want to pick up at the market, but Mom would not allow me because they were for "adults only." My pulse pounded in my ears and I stood there staring at him, breathless. *Dear lord . . . give me the strength.* I was playing with fire.

I peeled off the petal cups, and Nigel gasped. "Christ, love, you're going to be the death of me."

The bulge between his legs in his boxer briefs intimidated me.

"Do you know how beautiful you are?"

I shook my head "no," too self-conscious to come up with a response. This was the most intimate thing I'd ever done. Nigel made me feel beautiful and I wanted to share this bath with him. I trusted him though we'd only been dating for a month. Sex would have been easy.

All too easy. But I cared for Nigel more than anything, so why rush. He wasn't going anywhere. At least, I kept telling myself that.

"Are you sure you can do this? If it's too much—"

Nigel stood before me, inches away. "I'm fine."

It took all I had to keep my eyes on his face, as cute as that was. "You don't look like—"

"Just get in and be careful. It'll be slick because of the amount of oils you dumped."

"So if I slip it's my fault?" I chuckled.

"No, because I'm going to help you in. I won't let you fall."

Nigel took my arm and made sure I got in the tub without incident. I slid down into the warm water. He leaped over the edge and made it look graceful. He didn't disturb my mountain-high bubble cloud.

He took his time sinking down into the hot water. "I guess that's the answer to my question." Nigel laughed.

"What question?"

"You like it real hot."

There was no way I'd entertain that subject again. We were both trying to control ourselves. And god knew I was fighting some major impulses. Because the sad fact was that Nigel's build intimidated me.

"Tate, how do you like the tub?"

Everything was perfect. It helped that I couldn't see his body anymore because of the bubbles. Only that wet, wavy black hair was still teasing me. "The soak is very nice. I love it. Thanks."

Nigel sat up. "Could you see living here?" His shoulder muscles flexed.

"Oh, I would love a house like this."

"No. Could you see yourself in this house? Not another house like this one. This one?"

"What are you asking me?" Was he referring to the future? That far ahead? Zach had taught me one thing, never get ahead of yourself. Take one step at a time, because tomorrow your foot maybe broken. "Nigel, surely you're not thinking that far ahead?"

"Why not? Why can't I?"

"Well I guess you could, it's just—"

"What? You don't think we'll be together in years? Do you?"

I didn't answer. He was getting upset. I had been optimistic in the past, and it had burned me.

"Tatum? Look, I know I've only known you for just over a month, but you're different from anyone else I've ever met. That goes for here in the States and back in Surrey. When I think of not being with you, it drives me insane."

"Me too. I've thought about you like that. I've tried to imagine not being your girlfriend, and it breaks my heart."

He scooted forward, causing the bubble cloud to rise in front of me. We both chuckled, swiping the bubbles away.

"Jeez . . . did you have to pour in the bottle?" He laughed.

"Sorry. It is a bit insane."

"Tatum, hear me?"

I nodded. And with that, my heart began beating out of my chest. He was giving me that look again. But there was something different about his eyes. They were alive. Bright. Sincere.

"I love you."

He loved me? I glanced down at the bubble cloud. He brushed my hair out of my face. I met his stare and then it hit me—we were perfect for each other.

Taking in the appearance of his eyes, I felt it in my gut. But the damn fear ruled. This was my stupidity. This was what Zach and Kyle had done to me—made me afraid to trust guys. At least not for a long time.

Third time was the charm.

"I love you too, Nigel. I really do."

Nigel kissed me. I wrapped my arms around his shoulders and pulled him toward me. A lightning strike pulsated through my body. Nigel grabbed my foot and wrapped it behind his back. I let my other leg follow around his other side. With his arms wrapped around me, we both gave each other a little tug.

There was only one other way to be closer. That would be too easy with his excitement pressing against me. It was too close. Nigel made me forget about everything, except for what could happen if I let it.

I pulled away from his lips. "I do love you."

Nigel said nothing. He slid back, and I went to my side of the tub. With the most intense stare to my face, Nigel stood up, and bubbles slid down his body. There, at face level, was the most intimidating thing I'd ever seen in person. I had to look away. Dear lord . . . I had to look away to just be able to catch my breath.

Nigel grabbed the soap and lathered while he watched me. Soon he had no bubbles hiding anything on him. He sat down and rinsed off. "Here, turn around."

I did, not thinking twice. Nigel had my trust. I put my back to him. He swiped the hair off my shoulders and washed my back. He finished and planted a soft kiss on my shoulder. "I gotta get out. Sorry. But it's best if I keep my word to you."

Nigel didn't wait for a protest. He stood up and got out, then grabbed a bath towel.

One side of me didn't want him to get out. But the rational side knew he needed to. Damn it, we lasted a whole two minutes.

Nigel brushed his teeth at the sink and left the bathroom with the towel hung tantalizingly low.

With Nigel out of the bathroom, I could think clearly. I slid down into the water. Soaking in the tub with him was more exhilarating than I could have imagined. Even though we both pushed it, we did keep our word not to have sex.

I finished what I needed to and with my pajamas on, I met him in bed. He sat up with his back against a few pillows, arms behind his head, watching the TV in his boxers. He was so damn sexy.

I crawled in under the covers. He glanced over at me. "You smell good. I love that fresh shower smell."

"Me too. What you watching?"

"Just some Stooges. After *Saturday Night Live*, they always play them until like three in the morning."

I slid under the covers. The mattress was soft, but not too soft. My bones melted into the bed. Sleep was beginning to take over and I slid down on my pillow, not even watching the TV.

Nigel scooted down under the covers level to me and wrapped an arm around my waist. He whispered in my ear, "Tatum, if anything ever happens to us, like if we ever break up, I want you to agree you'll meet me at Dierbergs. On Saturday, April fourteenth, nineteen ninety."

That woke me up. "What? What are you talking about?"

"If we break up for any reason. Any. And you want to see me, or talk, or anything . . . you're to meet me there. I just can't imagine us apart. The thought kind of scares me."

"Nigel?" I sat up, resting my weight on my hand. "You clearly have a thing for planning ahead?"

He propped himself up on his arm and his hope-filled eyes searched my face. "Say you'll agree, Tatum. I can't go to sleep without this."

"Did you look at a calendar? How do you know April fourteenth is on a Saturday?" Nigel might have been going crazy, but I was fighting how cute he was.

"I glanced at a calendar, yes."

I had to force my stare to remain above the shoulders, which alone was challenging. "Okay. If something happens to us and we're not together . . . come April fourteenth this year, I will meet you at the deli department at Dierbergs. Agreed."

Nigel pulled me in an embrace. "Thanks. I love you, m'lady. Goodnight."

"I love you too, Nige. 'Night."

SUZIE T. ROOS

# COMING APRIL 2016:

# GIRL DEPARTS THREE

## SUZIE T. ROOS

An Excerpt from
**GIRL DEPARTS THREE**

Chapter 1

*Tatum*

*Monday, January 1, 1990*

The blazing sun on my tender eyes woke me. Muffled voices coming from inside the house made sure I was awake.

Nigel was lying inches away, with his back to me. Besides the beautiful black hair the only thing I could see was his muscular shoulders shaped into an impressive sculpture, reminding me just how lucky I was. Waking up with that view every morning was something I could get used to.

I carefully got out of bed and made my way to the bathroom to freshen up.

When I came back out, Nigel was sitting up in bed, watching TV again. "Morning, Tate. How did you sleep?"

"Good. The bed is comfortable. How about you?"

"I always sleep well in this house."

After Nigel took his turn in the bathroom, we put the

bedroom back together.

"Nige, what can I do out there to help clean up?"

"Nothing. Bren is staying with Anna, then Mom and Lester are coming over. We all clean and do laundry. Jessie and Tommy usually stay to help too."

"Wow, that's nice of everyone. If you're sure . . . I really don't mind cleaning."

"Nope. No need. There's more than enough hands on deck." He stepped close and caressed my shoulders. Another thing I could get use to was his hands on my skin of a morning. "Thanks for staying the night. I hope you had a good time."

"I did. It was the best. Besides, you told me you loved me for the first time. Nothing is better than that."

Nigel pulled me into his chest. "I do, you drive me mad."

"Well, the same goes for me too. You've been here for me. You're hot as hell. You're considerate and caring. You're everything, Nigel. What more can a girl ask for?"

Nigel and I had the bedroom and bathroom put back together and then he carried my duffel bag out to the garage door. He said goodbye to friends who were leaving while I found Andi and Di. They were finishing up in their bedroom.

I leaned against the doorframe, facing them. "Well, I guess I'm leaving soon. How 'bout you cats?"

They shoved the last bit in their bags and zipped up. With her bag in hand, Andi came up to me. "Tate, I have a big favor to ask of you."

Di rolled her eyes behind Andi.

"What is it?"

"Go to the airport with us?"

"Airport? For what?"

## GIRL DEPARTS THREE

"Hear me out. Matt is landing in a couple of hours. I've never even met his mom and dad before—"

"Nope. No can do. Sorry."

"Tatum." Andi grabbed my wrist. I jerked my arm, and she immediately released her hold. "Please? Look, you don't even have to say anything to them. They don't have to know you're even there. We . . . we can . . . go to the exit terminal. The big one before baggage claim. You can sit off to the side there. Di's coming."

Di passed us. "Yeah, you talked me into driving your ass."

I watched Di carry her bag out into the kitchen.

"Tatum, I beg you. Please?"

"Why?"

"I'll tell ya. Tate, you're not afraid of things. You deal with them. When you're with me, I can do things I wouldn't normally be able to do without you there."

I stood up all the way. "I'm not your mom. And I'm afraid of everything." After all the years, Andi still didn't know me. It was a front, because I pretended, using my imagination. It was easier than dealing with the reality of shitty things happening in my life.

"You? No, you're not."

Nigel joined us in the hall. "What's going on?"

"My boyfriend, Matt, is coming back home in a couple of hours. I'm trying to get Tate to go to the airport with me."

He scrunched up his face in confusion. "You don't want to go?"

If only Nigel understood what he was asking. I couldn't tell him who Matt's cousin was. Nigel would never let me near Andi alone again. Nigel and I had such a wonderful time together, why ruin it? "Not particularly."

"Well, Mum just got here with bagels and pastries. Whatever you decide, come eat first. I can still drive you home if you don't go with Andi."

Nigel walked back into the kitchen.

"Andi, don't. You know I can't tell him just yet who Matt's cousin is. Don't use Nigel as a pawn."

"Sorry, you're right. But I still want you to go with me. Otherwise I won't be able to see Matt until school tomorrow. Look, it's not like *he'll* be there."

"I don't care to see any Bertano, whether Zach would be there or not. You can see Matt in the morning, Andi. You can't possibly understand how it will affect me seeing any of his family. What if his parents are there? I can't take that chance."

Of course, I couldn't let her know the night before I'd overheard her telling Di that Zach slept with Mariacella, the Italian girl his Gramps was making him marry, and that he'd been sleeping around. Zach clearly did not love me anymore, let alone care about me. Not one phone call since he'd up and left me after Thanksgiving. No Christmas card. No message from his cousins. Nothing. I didn't want to be anywhere near the Bertano family. Zach didn't exist to me anymore.

"Andi, I can't." I walked toward the kitchen.

She followed me. "Dear god, Tatum. Please. I'm scared."

I spun around, and she nearly ran into me. "Give me one damn good reason why? And not because you say nothing scares me."

I noticed we had an audience in the kitchen. Jessie, Di, Nigel, Bren, and Anna stood frozen, watching me.

I lowered my head and voice. "Not here."

"Tate, what's the big deal, just go with her, love," Nigel said.

# GIRL DEPARTS THREE

I glared at Andi. She was putting me in a very unfortunate situation. Di stepped up and held my arm. "I'll be there. We'll stay off to the side. If I don't drive her there, she can't see him. Sounds like he has to do a family dinner when they get back, so she'll go with them. But you and I can leave as soon as she meets up with Matt."

I took a deep breath, looking like psycho of the year in front of everyone.

"I will owe you big time," Andi whispered. "Just come. You can leave when Matt gets there."

"You owe me big fucking time."

She threw her arms around my neck. "Oh, thank you. Thank you so much, Tate."

After we ate breakfast, the three of us headed out. Nigel walked me out to Di's car. He rested my back against the VW Rabbit. "I love you, m'lady. I'll call you tonight before bed. I have to go visit Grandpa Oscar. Mum and Lester make dinner at his house for New Years."

"That's nice. Tell Grandpa Oscar I said Happy New Year."

"Will do." Nigel kissed me goodbye.

Di warmed the car and Andi jumped in the back seat, letting me take the front.

I hopped in the car and Nigel's hands went into his pockets. "Drive safe. Talk tonight."

"I'll be waiting. Love you."

Nigel waved. "Love you too. Bye."

Di backed out of the driveway.

I rolled down the window and blew kisses at him. "Miss you already."

Di drove off. "You love him? Oh my gosh, Tate. That's awesome."

From the backseat, Andi reached up and patted my shoulder. "I'm so happy for you. Nigel's the best."

"He is. We had a great time before we went to bed last night."

"We heard the Jacuzzi going. I bet you had a good time." Di snickered.

"Believe it or not . . . we soaked in the tub filled with bubbles and just talked."

"Not," Andi shouted out, and laughed.

Di thought it was funny too.

"Well, we did. Now . . . not for long." They both chuckled. "But we did. I was kind of up front with him about not wanting to have sex. We agreed it was too easy to last night, so we would wait and let the tension build. Why rush?"

"Oh, you didn't?" Di said.

"What does that mean?"

"Do you know what it's like for a guy 'building tension,' forcing himself to not have sex?"

"Well, I'm sure like *us,* it's not easy. I just want to wait."

"You're scared he'll leave you like Zach did. I don't blame you."

"I am *not* afraid Nigel will *leave* me, Diane."

"Tate, she might be right. I know it's not what you want to hear, but if Zach didn't leave when he did, how much longer would you have waited with him?"

"Okay, forget I said anything at all. I'm not talking about my *relations* with you guys anymore."

Andi patted my shoulder and they both dropped it, which was for the best since I got worked up. I didn't want to take my frustration out on my girlfriends because of how Zach had left me. They didn't deserve that.

# GIRL DEPARTS THREE

Di turned on Lindbergh, one exit away from the airport. A short few minutes later and we pulled into the main terminal parking garage.

We entered through the level marked "Baggage Claim," and I took a seat on the bench against the wall. "Andi, you go up the ramp. I'll wait here."

The ramp was on the dim side since it was heading below ground level. At the top of the ramp, Lindbergh's plane, the *Spirit of St. Louis*, hung from the glass ceiling. Sunlight spilled down the ramp, but not all the way.

"Tate and I will wait here. And as soon as Matt shows, we'll take off."

"Okay, thanks again, Tate, for coming. I do appreciate it."

"Sure. Just remember you owe me. I'll let you know what it is when I come up with something good."

Di swatted my shoulder. "Tate, stop teasing her."

The speakers clicked on. "Flight two seventy-four from LaGuardia arriving at gate seven." The message repeated a second time.

"That could be them," Di said.

Andi looked back at us and smiled with thumbs up. I supposed that was their flight number.

I got comfy and rested my head on the wall. "I'm tired all of a sudden."

"Are you sure you got any sleep last night?"

I rolled my head to face her. "I did. But not the eight hours I require. It's stupid, but if I don't get at least eight hours, I'll yawn all day."

"You should take Vitamin B12."

"What does that do?"

"It helps your energy. Just try it, it can't hurt. It's a B vitamin."

"Hmm, I'll have to look into it." I rolled my head back and closed my eyes.

"Flight two seventy-four is arriving at gate seven. Luggage claim M-three." The announcement rang over the intercom.

"That's his flight, he's here," Andi called out.

I gave a thumbs up, not moving. I wanted to get home to take a nap.

We heard a bunch of voices with accents. I sat up and waited for Andi to spot Matt. Coming down the ramp was a group of people speaking Italian. No one Andi recognized yet. Maybe it was another family. The Bertanos weren't the only Italians.

"Matt?" Andi screeched.

Di and I both jumped. "Jesus, did she have to scream?" I said.

Matt dropped his bag and ran for Andi. Lifting her in the air and spinning her around, he kissed all over her face. It was sweet how much he'd clearly missed her.

Then I watched a middle-aged couple stopped at Andi and Matt. The guy, who was as big as Andre the Giant, said, "Matt? Is this your Andi?"

"Yeah, this is her. Andi, this is my mom and dad."

They exchanged pleasantries. Matt's mom grabbed Andi and hugged her, welcoming her to the family.

"Jesus, Di . . . look at how big that guy is," I whispered.

"Now we know where Matt gets it from."

"Yeah." I laughed. "No joke. I'm ready to go. You?"

"Yeah, he's here now. Let's take off," Di said.

We grabbed our purses and headed toward the parking garage.

"I'm glad you made it. Who drove you?" Matt said.

I could just hear him.

"Di and Tatum did. Bye, guys. Thanks again," Andi called out.

Di and I waved, but kept going. I didn't want to have to talk to any of them. And I sure as hell wasn't meeting a Bertano today, if ever.

"Matt? You okay?" Andi asked.

"Shit. Why did you bring Tatum?"

I refrained from flipping Matt off, although I really wanted to.

"What the hell is his problem?" Di whispered.

"No clue. Nor do I care, but look at the thanks I get."

"Oh shit, that's Tatum? Why is she here," we heard Matt's father say.

That did it, I did care. I stopped. Di followed my lead. We both turned around to see what their problem was.

The moment I looked up the ramp, I saw him standing there, frozen, his bag at his side.

Zach.

# ABOUT THE AUTHOR

Suzie T. Roos is from, and has settled in, St. Louis with her husband, two children and a number of foster pets at any given time.

She and her husband have lived everywhere from Philadelphia, PA to out West in Santa Monica, Ca. They're thankful they could expose their children to different American lifestyles and cultures.

Besides writing, Suzie's hobbies include movies, traveling, and especially concert going her husband and friends.

She's always been an animal lover and animal rights advocate. She is certified by FEMA in IS-00011.a Animal in Disasters: Community Planning. She's also an active volunteer at the Humane Society of Missouri.

Connect with Suzie T. online:
Website: www.suzietroos.com
Email: suzietroos@yahoo.com
Twitter: @SuzieTRoosbooks
Facebook: www.facebook.com/SuzieTRoos
Sign up for new release updates at:
http://www.suzietroos.com/contact.html